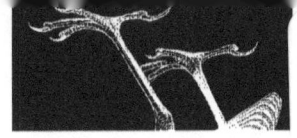

I0652994

Final State

www.finalstatepress.com

The End is the Beginning

& other stories

Matt Briggs

Also by Matt Briggs:

The Remains of River Names
Misplaced Alice
The Moss Gatherers
Shoot the Buffalo

The End is the Beginning

& other stories

Matt Briggs

Also by Matt Briggs:

The Remains of River Names
Misplaced Alice
The Moss Gatherers
Shoot the Buffalo

To LVP

The author would like to thank the following magazines, Web sites, and community bulletins where some of these stories have previously appeared: *The Clackamas Literary Review, First Intensity, The Jack Straw Anthology, The Raven Chronicles, Mississippi Mud, The Mississippi Review, Smokelong Quarterly, Seattle Magazine, The Steel City Review, Semantikon, Slouch Magazine,* and *The Wandering Hermit Review.*

The author would like to thank the curators of reading series where he first read many of these stories including Esther Helfgott at It's About Time; Doug Nufer at Titlewave's New Reading Series and A Leg to Stand On; Rebecca Brown at the Brontësaurous; Paul Hunter and Steve Potter at Red Sky; and Bret Lunsford and Rich Jensen at What the Heck Fest.

Final State Press
finalstatepress.com

The End is the Beginning

Contents

The Plague of Fur

The Plague of Fur began, as such things do, with a faint smudge of peach fuzz. The fur, once invented, contained the capacity to grow and spread. Like all life, it wanted to make more of itself. The fur originally grew behind doors sealed with an airlock. The fur grew in vats placed in a vault. For several months after it had been invented, the substance thrived in its contained environment, pushing, spreading, and waiting for a hole to appear where it could spread through the world.

A postal carrier contracted the fur from the lobby of an engineering firm in a new building overlooking Lake Union in Seattle on the Pacific Coast of North America. The architect had added accents of exposed timber to the concrete and rebar frame. The timber was composite wood similar in most respects to fiberboard except the process made the timbers look whole and natural, and they were in fact, stronger than natural timber. The fiber had been

engineered to carry structural strength. Construction
has long entered the realm of the invisible. A building
begins with molecules and ends with microfiber, static-
free carpets. Entering the building the postal carrier felt
as if he had entered a rustic hunting lodge with exposed
beams; antique (period) kayaks hung from the rafters;
a collection of historic snow shoes clung to the massive
wall behind the front desk. Display lights beneath each
pair made a massive wall of glowing, wicker butterflies.
A lab technician, dismissed from his prior position in a
blood cancer lab for not washing his hands, had worked
in the nanolab behind the lobby. Repeating his behavior
he carried the invisible, mechanical life form, a self-
replicating filament, from the lab, and into the lobby. He
left a coating of wool in the mailroom. During the day as
everyone checked their mail, they contracted the fuzz and
carried it into their varous networks of contact.

The fur began as a test to make something that could
assemble itself from readily acquired molecules: H_2O and
CO_2. The factory was much smaller than a head of a pin;
in fact, it was so small it would take a hundred-thousand
factories to cross the width of a pin. A cluster of these
factories began as a thin layer and then began to assemble
itself more and more rapidly into lattice strands that grew
from several micros to a millimeter (where on careful
inspection it could be seen with the naked eye) and in
several minutes began to appear to be a fur just as mold
appears to be a fur. However, the lattice structures could
support columns that grew to a dozen or more centimeters
long. This looked like classic animal fur. As the strands
grew in length, the weight of the fiber grew too heavy for
the lattice support and then cleaved into another section.
The broken strand in turn could find purchase on most
surfaces. The base, a mess of microscopic roots would fill
nearly any surface. The broken strand then grew back to

the full length before becoming too heavy and breaking again. In this way, the fur spread. To see the fur spread across the room was like watching someone scribble in slow motion. Gradually the surfaces began to grow thick with strands, and then finally the entire room was a dense, fuzzy clump. It began as nothing that could be seen, a smear of microscopic particles, and it ended in fur.

By the time the postal carrier had reached the end of his shift, he had left peach fuzz on his letters and hair grew on his truck. He looked into the rearview mirror, and he was unsure what was growing on him. Back at the postal center, he went to the nurse. The nurse examined him and said there was something growing on him, but he didn't know what it was. Fungus?

The fur, in an abundant quantity, was ice colored. It was translucent and turned bluish or whitish depending on the light coming down against it. In the lab, it appeared mostly silver and white.

During the day, buildings seeded by the carrier began to gain fur and then by the end of the evening, the fur had spread through Seattle. Fuzz traveled on the freeway north to Vancouver BC, South to Los Angeles, East to Missoula. The block along Lake Union where it had first escaped was covered with a thick layer of fur that looked like snow, except as snow it covered vertical walls, it covered the area under the roofs, it covered trees, it covered animals, and it continued to spread at a steady pace: a meter a minute.

First, the fire department was called and came, but they walked around the fur and the fur began to grow on them. They called an ambulance. There was nothing they could do. They called the Army. The Army sent a team from ReCon. Troops mobilized and began to collect at Fort Lewis, the base south of Tacoma.

The team arrived twelve hours after the technician

seeded the mailroom. Lt. Col. Sarah Fog wore short gray hair and a pair of bluish BDUs with an orange HAZMAT badge on the shoulder. From the air, as Fog approached she could see the news helicopters like fruit flies flying around a puddle of apple cider vinegar. The incident from the air was beautiful; the strands of fur from a thousand feet glittered and sparkled like an oil slick. It comprised a disc covering, now, twenty city blocks. One margin ended at Lake Union, and the other progressed up the hills around the lake. Fog could see new incidents of growth occurring in other areas of the city where traffic through the site had carried fur. It followed patterns like cancer: metastasis. Smaller but sizable dots grew at intersections and coffee shops. In turn, any traffic moving through these clumps would contract fur and carry it deeper into the city.

Reports began to come in from cities up and down Interstate-5 that there were growths. "Call central command," Fog said. "This growth must be contained."

It was dusk, and traffic was diverted from the area, and as a result, traffic moved at a crawl through the entire Puget Sound basin. The growth continued unabated and in fact accelerated as a result of the sluggish movement of cars.

The ReCon team had to capture a sample and so the helicopter landed in an empty parking lot. On the ground, things were different. The evacuation of the blocks around the growth had gone well. The team landed in the middle of an occupied and full city at rush hour, and yet walking down the block it seemed they were alone. The soldiers knew this feeling from doing drill. They came to the end of the block and in front of them, there it was, the world covered in fur. The fur grew from lampposts, along the curbs, from the rims of tires. Fog, in full hazmat gear (gas mask, rubber boots, charcoal cover layer) advanced on the plague and then extracted a sample. She drew the sample back, placed it into a sealed container. She retreated. The fur grew while she watched until it filled the container.

She advanced to the helicopter and discarded her gear on the sidewalk. The team decontaminated her. She climbed into the helicopter, and the team flew to the Command Center set up on Blake Island in Puget Sound.

It had been noted that it did not grow on water. During the night, they analyzed the growth and discovered then the molecule sized factories that created the strands. This was a deliberate synthetic organism.

It wasn't life, but it was really close. They held their fingers together, gallows humor, because what is the different if live ends on earth from something manufactured or a virus or a natural disaster? Life will still end. They were relieved because working in a rapid response Hazmat team, they often wondered how the world would end. They dreamed of the world's end and their futile, though noble battle against the horror of a plague that would leave bodies in the streets of the cities. To think, the world would end in fur. It was a relief to know.

Puzzling, though, was that the people with fur growing on them, about two hundred people they rounded up from the initial site who were in a contained unit with an air lock in a building surrounded by barbed wire, they were alive even though they were covered, mostly in fur. It didn't grow in their nostrils. It didn't grow in their eyes or mouth.

What was more puzzling was that several of the patients could not be stopped from eating the fur.

It wouldn't grow on water. And during that night they found that the fur would dissolve in water and turn into a simple sugar.

They sprayed the fur with water, and it dissolved.

They sent the report.

During the night it rained, and the rain cleaned Seattle, mostly. The next day a steady drizzle fell and kept the fur down.

The fur still clung to dry places and as the rain abated, and sidewalks began to dry again the fur began to regrow. Within the month, fur grew in every major West Coast city and had shown up in every major world city. Fur covered the artic ice. In Seattle, by the end of the month fur grew inside everyone's car and inside everyone's houses.

The novelty of fur-covered buildings soon wore off. People worked to remove the fur, and then once a building had been defurred the occupants installed the *Bald Protocol*. A defurring chamber was built. Items were carried in hard plastic shells and sprayed with water. People removed outside clothes and showered and then put on new building clothes, with a badge that said they had been cleaned.

Hair, already unpopular, became even more unpopular. Everyone shaved all of the hair off their bodies so that it was clear they didn't have the beginnings of the plague. Furless animals appeared in houses.

A lack of fur became a sign of wealth and hospitality.

Only the poor remained with hair and fur. Their houses were covered in fur. Their bodies were furry. Sayings began to circulate, "The fur is always with us." Or if you met someone on the street, you might say of them, "He's furry," implying they were low class.

During dry spells fur spread from the crevices where it had flourished. The city kept a fur watch.

Many cities employed defurriers who waited for the dry spells to find catches of fur. They trolled the neighborhoods with water trucks and sprayed away any occurrence of fur.

A president was elected who said he would clean

the nation of fur. For four years, brigades of defurriers removed fur. For a time at the end of his presidency, it seemed that fur had been removed. Even the poor were no longer furry. Fur had been driven into the wilderness and out of the cities. The period when fur was commonly was called *The Time of Fur*. The fur rescinded into dry caves. And when the fur was finally, officially, eradicated, it left the world bald and empty. Such was progress.

Jason Johansson: Mute

With the increase in the world's population (more people are alive right this minute than have been alive throughout history) and the spread of the English tongue, the totality of original utterances has begun to drop to unprecedented lows. At one point when the total population of English speakers was close to two million in the sixteenth century, nearly any sentence uttered by a speaker had a good chance of having never been spoken before. To talk about your neighbor's odors was to engage a bold, new linguistic enterprise. Now it has come to the point that we can only discus such matters using the recycled, previously uttered phrases of days gone by. Jason Johansson calculated that on May 11th, 2027, the last truly unique sentence will be uttered. Then, excluding lexical mutations and the introduction of technology-based concepts, all of the possible permutations of English will have been exhausted.

Nothing bored Johansson as much as the repetition of his aunt's stories. On visits to his apartment, his aunt quickly entered her routines about the cruelty inflicted on her by her so-called friends, by the indignities inflicted on her by her co-workers. Tormenters all. Substitute a name here and there, the syntax of her routine remained the same. In school, the teachers inflicted a similar torture on poor Johansson's sensitive nature. A haiku is nothing except a cookie-cutter path to fruit petals on a branch, transcendental clichés, and monotonous doggerel.

The world he calculated would soon fall into a Dark Age. All of the languages had been absorbed into English. No longer would there be those moments of liberation when English raided Latin or French or Spanish. The world would fall into a Dark Age of repetition after 2027 when even the liberating mechanisms of juxtaposition and irony could not save every spoken word from following the tiresome clichés, the repetitions of past originality, a beating to death of the jokes, the complete exhaustion of language.

Johansson relinquished language, settling on a crude sequence of gestures to declare his bodily necessities. He renounced language but retained the gesture for water, food, and toilet paper. Gradually his thoughts, even, emptied of language. When 2027 came, he sat on a chair in the sun on his damp lawn. The sun was warm, but he did not think that; he only thought that he did not desire movement.

Edgar

The last thing I shredded, his birth certificate, jammed the machine. Pretty frills stuffed the margins. The shredder's teeth tangled in the thick cream bond. The only thing that made that certificate appropriate for Edgar was that it had been typed out on a crooked typewriter. The *e* twisted so that the next letter got stamped over it. That one screwed-up thing made the whole official paper look as if a juvenile scam artist had slapped it together. I must admit I felt crappy after I pulled out the confetti that had been his birth certificate. Edgar had been really proud of his weight printed on that paper. Thirteen pounds, thirteen hours of labor. He was a skinny little guy back when we first started to hang out on account of his problems. As soon as he started to put down my cooking, things got better for him. He must have weighed over three hundred pounds when he died. Considering how many pounds of flour, sugar, butter, and cocoa powder

I'd turned into cake and he'd turned into lard, I felt bad about what I'd done to him.

I carted Edgar outside with his own dolly and cut him up into barrel-sized chunks. I used to pull my kid brother's action figures apart, two arms, two legs, a torso, and a head. To keep out the flies, I wrapped each one up in a Hefty garbage bag, double ply, the kind Edgar would never let me buy. Instead of flies, clouds of wasps flew out from the field. I had to wear Edgar's old gloves, still reeking of his work sweat, to keep from getting stung by the swarm hunting down fresh meat. I hefted his head up with two hands and dropped it into the burn barrel. I stuffed newspaper around his skull and poured in five gallons of gasoline. The yellow jackets rushed out and then flew in lazy circles in the fumes. I let the whole thing soak for about an hour. When I got back, hundreds of sated, drunk wasps rested on the lip of the barrel. I dropped a match into the can. The vapors ignited before the match even reached the paper. The yellow jackets, the wads of the daily, Edgar's head, everything went up.

If I could have found a poison that would have made Edgar just vanish, things would have been much easier. Instead, I had to extract him from my life one piece at a time. I removed his breath with a heavy doze of strychnine-laced red velvet cake. He asked, "What's the occasion?" As soon as he said this, the gigantic drunk thug who had been my husband became that sweet, skinny man I had first met so many years ago.

I wore a yellow sundress and white sandals on our first date. I should have seen everything coming, then. I'd just cut my hair when I stopped to admire myself in a junk shop window. I stood out on the sidewalk in the full daylight. I caught my reflection in the glass under the pawnshop awning and I noticed in that image that Edgar had this fierce scowl and that a pack of sailors in their dress whites stood on the street corner and were looking our way. They were looking at me. I took Edgar's hand and kissed him on the cheek and his face went all limp and I said, "Come on." As soon as we came to the Arcade, I had him play *The Lover's Challenge*, to take out some of his anger. He throttled the lever and sent the *Love o' Meter* sailing against the bell. Another sailor walked down the pier by himself, saw us at the machine and stopped. There was something familiar about him, a familiar nose or something. He took off his little round cap and rolled it into a ball and started to walk toward us.

"Let's go," I said.

"I'm not finished playing."

I yanked his arm and held it against my side as we hurried up First Avenue past the long green newspaper stand crowded with men in overcoats paging through the foreign newspapers. The sailor followed us to the market and stopped at the rack and bought himself a paper. The Public Market smelled like damp lettuce, mushrooms, raw fish, and gasoline. Slowly walking bodies, grandfathers showing out-of-town grandchildren the city, kindergartners linked one hand to the next, jumbled all together so it was a big pedestrian traffic jam. The sailor eased against a timber pillar, letting the walkers pass him, watching Edgar and me stop at a fruit vendor. Edgar bought me three pounds of black cherries. He handed the man a crumpled bill, and the man handed back a creased, brown paper bag full of black fruit. I grabbed the bag and rushed down a staircase and into a dim, smoky spice shop. Tiny packages of curry, masala, and strange colored beans stuffed the shelves. The store was warm and empty. "No," Edgar said when I offered him a cherry. "They make me sick." We passed down a narrow hallway and then behind the craft stalls. We could see the backs of the vendors. A man sat on a milk crate reading a paperback. "You know your way around," Edgar said.

"Yes, I do." I had a cherry pit in my mouth. When we came out onto the balcony, we were alone and I spit the stone down into the grassy green belt between the Alaskan Viaduct and the Market.

"Let's sit down," Edgar said.

We sat on a knoll overlooking the stream of loud traffic on the viaduct, Puget Sound glittering with waves, and the distant blue heaps of the Olympic Mountains. I ate my cherries, all three pounds of them, spitting the pits down into the blackberries. I wanted, then, Edgar to kiss me, there in privacy. It was just us and all around us the city moved; trucks and buses moved on the highway, ferries and sailboats moved on the water, and the thin trails of jets drifted in the stratosphere. We both sat on Edgar's jacket. I would have leaned right over then and kissed him except he had a long twist of a grass stalk in his mouth. He whirled one finger around and pulled the length of it taut with his teeth. He plucked a single chord over and over again. Finally, he noticed my head bent toward him, pulled the stalk free, and he kissed me. I felt a little sick. I had never felt like that kissing a boy before. I felt a heavy, burning weight in my stomach. It wanted to come out, one way or the other. "I need to go to the bathroom. I don't feel well."

"You shouldn't have wolfed those cherries down," Edgar said. "It's a waste of money to gobble them up if they are just going to come right out again."

On the way back into the market, the sailor found us coming up the steps. "There you are," he said. "It is you, isn't it?"

"You have her mistaken for somebody else," Edgar said. "She needs to use the can."

I realized on the stairs then, seeing the sailor from under

him, he was a kid I used to know from church a long time ago. The sailor wouldn't move from the stairs and before I could say anything, on account of me just trying to hold that burning knot of black cherries in one place in my stomach, Edgar said, "Just because she's a lady doesn't mean she's a whore." He punched the sailor in the face. I just about lost all of those cherries, and I rushed past those two boys and was sick in the bathroom. When I had rinsed my mouth out, the taste of my stomach was still sharp and hard on my tongue, I didn't want to come out and see that boy from church all beat up, or worse, I didn't want to come out and see Edgar all beat up. After counting to five hundred, I did come out. Edgar was the only one there. He smiled and looked just as wiry and fresh as when he picked me up that morning. He took my hand and we walked back to his car. I felt something damp on my hand and looked down and saw that his knuckles were bleeding all over me. I should have seen the clues right then. Those things, him saying *can* like that, him hitting the sailor just like that, they seemed like things that just happened. They didn't, at that time, tell me the things I needed to worry about.

He turned my red velvet cake around on the glass cake plate. Edgar reached out to taste the red velvet cake icing on the tip of his pointer finger. I said, "I think I am finally going to move. I think I have the strength." Even as I said this, I started to get regrets, you know like you do when things are already happening the way you planned, but you think maybe they were better the way they were?

"Honey, you ain't going nowhere. Get me some milk so I can enjoy your cake." I poured him a glass. He guzzled it down and gobbled his first piece of cake right up.

My mother was in love with Edgar. She believed all the lies he had built around himself. Well, they weren't lies exactly, because he did do these big nice things just like he did those big not-so-nice things. Which side of a guy like Edgar is the real one? Did he do the good things to conceal who he really was? One year, when the factory laid people off, Edgar bought the uniforms for the kids' team. Did he do the nasty things to conceal who he really was? Last year when I got sick, he carried me down to the basement and I didn't see him for a month. I sat down there in the dark and cold, sweating and hollering until I thought I'd die down there. To Edgar's credit, he did leave me a flat of plastic Evian bottles and a trash-sized bag of popcorn from Costco. When I finally regained the strength to crawl out of that bed and claw my way up the stairs back into the warm kitchen, I heard him call out from the living room, "Who in the hell is that? Oh, it's you." My mother didn't know anything about Edgar. She didn't know where his money came from and didn't care because he had money and he went to church. When I told my mother about Edgar's threat to kill me if I left him, my mother just said, "Don't be a fool. They stopped making men like Edgar a long time ago and I don't think they are planning on starting up again. You have yourself a genuine historical artifact."

Everyone sure loved Edgar. When I told the hairdresser that he had left me, they all started to call, I think more to find out where he had gone to than to express any real consideration about my feelings. My story went: I spent the weekend at my mother's house and when I came home, the front door was unlocked and Edgar wasn't there. They all said, "Are you all right, honey? Can I bring you anything until he turns up." They speculated about what had happened to him right down to me murdering him and getting rid of his body, but the only thing that could tell them anything was that old burn barrel out in the middle of the field. And it wasn't saying anything, because before I went over to my mother's house, I took a trip to the county dump and got ride of some things. When I came back into Edgar's house, sat down in the kitchen and looked at the empty shelves behind the cupboards the wind had blown open in the changing weather, I knew no one was coming home anymore.

My Gruesome Death

My head fit in the gap between the wheels of the dump truck. I imagined if I put my head there, the tires would force my skull between the tires like a pebble between two cogs, to the pavement, where the rear tires would run me over crushing my braincase into pulp. The cause and effect of it became something I couldn't stop thinking about. I would do it.

A white walking figure flashed in the pedestrian box. I could cross. The dump truck and its trailer pulled forward faster and faster, and then they were gone. I was certain the next time I saw them, I would do this: I would place my head between the wheels of the dump truck.

My gradeschool teachers had often dressed me down for my imagination. "You have a great head on your shoulders," Ms. Ledford told me. I couldn't tell whether my great head was a desirable thing or something to fix, so I smiled, "Thanks," I said.

"It's always the quiet ones," she said.

"Always what?" I wondered. "What do you mean?"

Thoughts came to me unbidden. Sometimes they were confirmation of how wonderful the world was. The moon was a hole in the sky and through it I could see the other world from where we have fallen.

I caught a glimpse of the back of my head in the reflective appliance store mirror. Scarcely no one had as bumpy a head as I had. Trucks rumbled on the street. They were the kind that moved significant portions of the earth from one site to another. Heavy trucks moved land to the hills near my home where they were building a third runway to the airport. On the high-speed freeway near my home, there were always dump trucks moving dirt. A tailor-made exit had been tailored for them.

Rather than drive the route home past the third runway construction, I went to the movies. I wanted to find a substitute image to displace the thought of my head placed between the two wheels. Coming home from the movies I was distracted by the conversation of people leaving the multiplex. Someone said, I thought she was beautiful. Such a dramatic chase! The action was so intense as though I was strapped to my seat and being beaten with a rubber pipe in the face. No one I know has such a bumpy head. What's-his-name was excellent. A real star. Unforgettable. If I had been tortured the way he had been tortured I would have confessed to anything you imagined: I wear a dress; I killed my mother; whatever. They brought out the toothpicks. He was so stoic and well dressed. I would give my left arm for biceps like his.

I was struck by the roundness of the tires, the perfect fit of my head in the gap between them and the idea of my head even for a second rolling between them. Any idea once had wouldn't go away, but was there no matter how nonsensical. Other ideas like this had descended on me before. They wouldn't go away until I did something about them. They would drive me mad unless I did something about them. I preferred they not be unhealthy ideas as this one was clearly unhealthy. I didn't want to die. But, once something is made, even an idea, it cannot be unmade. An idea must be displaced.

"Such a head on your shoulders," Ms. Ledford had said. Ledford kissed the boys on their birthdays. She wore copious applications of make up, possessed two poodles whose activities supported her anecdotal asides addressing the themes of immorality and the carnal nature of our biological existence. I was only ten and Ms. Ledford seemed inordinately ancient and wrinkled and overdressed. Her silky blouses in lush floral hues: pale green, lavender, and iris blue emitted a soft sound as she trolled the classroom. Ledford tottered on towering shoes with elaborate buckles and straps. They clacked on the linoleum classroom floor. She smelled of leather and roses. I associate the odor with deodorizers intended to conceal the smell of rot. Ledford saw an older man named Svenson, an executive at a downtown bank. On occasion, Svenson turned up at the end of the day with a bouquet. Ledford carried them away with her holding them in front her as if they would suddenly spill from their wrap and shatter on the floor. Svenson's silent, adoring presence leant authority to my teacher's exegesis on the carnal nature of our biological existence.

I couldn't stop thinking about the dump truck wheels. On the stroll through the multiplex parking lot to my car I kept looking for them. On the drive home, I passed the construction of the third runway and there were plenty of trucks. The problem though was that they weren't stopping. I needed them to have stopped so I could safely lay my head between the tires.

They were burying swamps and a tiny stream under

a mountain of soil trucked in a steady traffic of dump trucks. Even two years ago, the tiny stream bore salmon. I walked in the forest between the freeway and highway and clogged arterials. I could hear the stop-and-go traffic until the trail cut into the steep gulley dug by the flow of water. The odor of dead fish, the silence of the deep forest, dripping water from moss, the patter of water from a shallow waterfall filled the gulley. Downstream from the soil, the gulley would die. The dump-truck soil contained cyanide. All dirt in the West contained cyanide. Everything had been stripped for gold, tin, plastic.

I would place my head between the tires and pull it back before it started again, thereby fulfilling this image, sparing my life, and discharging the image. I would return home and take a bath in scalding water.

I drove against the traffic of dump trucks. They came in a steady line from the east along a highway that connected to the highway I took home. The highways intersected at an overpass adjacent to a defunct International House of Pancakes that had been converted to other uses. Now it was a Thai Restaurant. I parked in the lot. I observed the trucks at the intersection. They idled at the light. It was a long light. I timed it: two minutes.

Inside the International House of Pancakes Thai Restaurant lobby, a wooden elephant raised its trunk. The place smelled of the warm odor of the kitchen: curry, coriander, and tea. Star-shaped paper lanterns hung from the Bavarian style rafters of the building. A golden Buddha sat with his legs crossed gazing pacifically over the diners. "You may sit anywhere," the hostess said. I sat at a booth with a view of the dump trucks. I ordered beef in coconut milk curry. It was delicious. As a possible last meal it was a suitable culinary high point. It was flavorful and a little too spicy in a way that I like things to be a little too spicy. Every bite reminded me I was eating. A rain began to fall, flinging tiny flecks of water against the window. It wasn't major enough to even warrant people turning on their wipers. The daylight began to fade. The streetlights were off. It was very dark outside. It was darker than it would be when the streetlights came on.

After I charged my bill and tipped well to ensure goodwill I walked along the sidewalk to the overpass. Three trucks with trailers sat at the light. I crossed and watched them go pass the light two at a time. And then, just as it was dark, the streetlights flashed on.

I would be seen whether anyone looked, but on the busy overpass with rush hour traffic below me, with a long line of cars waiting to turn one way or another I was in the wilderness. The overheated engines emitted the scent of burnt oil and tailpipe carbon. I couldn't see inside the cars to the people. Squat hemlock grew in the median. The cement overpass collected puddles of water. A breeze carried flecks of rain. The air vibrated with the pitch of traffic on the highway below, on the overpass, and the airplanes moving through the clouds.

A dump truck pulled to the light. Two minutes and I would be free.

I jumped down and lay my head so that my ears brushed the rubber. It was surprisingly warm from the friction of highway travel. It was pleasantly warm. I felt my head thus encased in the warm, hard rubber or whatever it was that they made tires out of now. Efficiency had replaced all of the old materials with surprising substitutes. There weren't even bits of gravel or other sharp substances lodged into the tires. Sensually it was better than I had wished. Just as I started to pull my head back, the wheels turned. My head was a cog. My entire body wrenched as the motion carried my head down.

And that was all I remembered for some time. One could assume if I were telling this as a story that I had died and that perhaps this story you are reading was in the manner of "Occurrence at Owl Creek Bridge" where Ambrose Bierce reveals that the entire tale up to that point was in the narrator's mind just as he was being hung. He was dead, so how could he tell you a tale? Dead men tell no tales, or so the pirates say. In this case, it would be me telling the story and this would be the story right before my desire was consummated with my head crushed under the warm rubber or whatever substitute substance the tires are made of these days.

On the boys' birthdays Ledford applied a second, a third, a fourth layer of bright-red lipstick. She pinned the boys down and left clots of blood colored lipstick on our cheeks. The image of my teacher's ritual ended not with her, but a pre-adolescent boy with a matronly, lipstick-kiss embossed on his cheek. No one wanted to be kissed by Ms. Ledford. Nearly all of the boys grudgingly struggled and then took the buss and left it on their cheek to show around class before rubbing it off. They were good sports about it. I, however, had taken the struggle for granted. I would prevent my cheek having any kind of lipstick-kiss embossed on it. The boys in the class tried to grab me. I ran. They had corned me in the back of the room and struggled to lift me. I managed to gain my feet again. I lowered myself, so the boys tumbled on my back. Their breath smelled of lunchtime milk and tater tots. I flung them off me. Boys fell against desks, against the walls, and I jumped free. "Calm down!" Ledford said. I thought she was about to relent, but the boys grabbed me again. My feet lost contact with the linoleum. I squirmed, and she planted her soft, greasy lips against my cheek. Even then I wiggled so much the normal-kiss-shaped buss smeared into a long gash down my neck. I knocked my teacher's glasses to the floor. Everything broke up as the boys looked for them and found them unbroken under the hamster cage. I was disappointed later examining the mark in the bathroom that it didn't match the other boys. After that struggle, there was no way I could get a do over.

When I woke, I sat against the side of the cabin inside the truck. My neck hurt. Also, I wasn't dead.

A man in overalls, a neatly pressed white shirt, a hat with a round brim drove the truck. I was inside of the dump truck. He turned to me. "Why do you do this?" I could see the black hair of his legs through holes in his trousers. A burr of unraveled thread rimmed his collar. Some food rested in a wedge between the glass, and the glove box, two slices of bread, it looked, with a smear of butter and a bruised Red Delicious.

"Where am I?" I asked.

"Crushing your head under on my truck. Don't make your insanity my business."

We drove along a ramp through a muddy region, and then he stopped. The truck vibrated. He pulled a shiny black handle attached to a lever. The entire truck shook. The odor of fresh earth infused the cab. I looked around us, but could just see two lamps with rain falling down into the light. Judging from the shadows, the truck was on some kind of bridge. And then, he ratcheted the truck into gear and began to drive again.

"You value your life?"

"I guess I am glad to be alive," I said. "Thank you." I had never said this to anyone before, aside from my mother: "I owe you my life."

"I just happened to look up," he said, "and seen your head in my tires. In stopping, the tires do a quarter turn back and that caused your head to pop up. If I had stepped on the gas, as I was about to do, you would be dead."

"Thank you, again. Would it be any trouble—"

"That's worth something."

"It is," I said. "I would give you five hundred dollars in cash if I had it. I'd give you more."

"What do you have?"

"I don't have enough to repay you in kind," I said.

"Anything would be a help," he said.

"You have my thanks," I said. "Anything."

"What amount of money can you give me?"

"I have two hundred dollars in my account. How about that?"

He shook and gripped the steering wheel until his knuckles seemed white against the black plastic. "Okay. Okay. We'll stop at a machine."

"Can you stop at my bank, Puget Sound Thrift? I'd like to avoid the finance charge."

"I can't drive city streets," he said. "There is another bank just off the ramp."

"That's where my car is."

"Dead, you wouldn't have any use for a car."

"I'm not dead," I said.

"You would be," he said. "If I hadn't—"

I found my cell phone in my pocket. I pulled it out to show him I still had connections among the living.

"Isn't your life worth more than your car?"

I felt as I had been given my life. Alive there was a lot I could do with 200 dollars. I didn't have to pay my bills this month. I could buy the Bob Dylan box set and round out my collection in a snap. I could rent a room with a sauna tub. I could get myself something nice.

He parked the trailer in the lot of the International House of Pancakes Thai Restaurant. I didn't point out my car. We walked to the crosswalk, and then along the busy street. We walked across to the bank.

"How about you run a balance first?" he asked me.

"Forget it," I said. "This isn't going to work. You keep wheedling me."

"Okay. 200 bucks."

"Thanks for saving my life. That's what my life is worth," I said, "my eternal thanks." It was worth this.

"You owe me."

"No," I said. "I don't."

I didn't want to say anything more on the matter. We stood on the sidewalk in the glow of the cash machine monitor. I watched him think it through. For a second, it looked he was going to sock me. He was going to do something because he stood completely still with his arms down at his side. Through the holes in his trousers, I could see his legs had turned pink. I didn't have any thought about putting my card into the machine, or even taking my wallet out of my back pocket. I clutched my cell phone and waited, and I remembered the rubber or whatever substance those tires were made out of. I had displaced the thought with a memory, and I was grateful for that much, to have nice things to think about. "Which way back to my truck? I wasn't paying attention," he said. I looked around as well, unsure of where we were in the dark.

The End is the Beginning

Stage 1: Warning

My mailbox was flattened that October, not like mailbox baseball, but flattened like a steamroller had passed over the metal post, leaving it crushed into the clover and gravel growing in the no-man's-land between the curb and the fence edging my yard.

My first thought was that I had enemies that I didn't know about. The enemies lurked in front of their plasma TV screens with the curtains drawn. Only the faint blue light leaked out at the edges of their drapes. I lived near a highway that is often described in the local media as "an abandoned strip of highway." As if even the traffic that pours across the highway isn't really aware of where it is passing, as if even though this strip of highway passes through decades-old planned unit developments, edged with unfinished furniture stores and motels, it is still wilderness.

This was another thought: *my crushed mailbox was a warning*.

I began to look for whoever had committed this crime against me. The mailbox itself had been targeted. There weren't tire tracks. A drunk driver would have left tracks. A drunk driver would have been unable to hit the target with such precision. The fence would have been damaged. Less malicious activity would have left evidence.

In a short period of time, though, an epidemic of other apparently unrelated acts swept the neighborhood. I ignored the signs because I do not believe in prophecies.

A swarm of possums gushed down the middle of the street at ten-thirty Wednesday morning. The entire street filled with slick and furry white bodies with pink noses. Where the possums came from and where they went I don't know. Many were hit on the abandoned strip of highway. Their carcasses attracted swarms of crows. For several days the din was unbearable.

In the middle of the night, half my neighbors disappeared. Since I wasn't aware of their activity, their disappearance didn't alarm me until their dogs went unfed. Three days after the event—marked only by the darkness in the evening as plasmas TVs were not turned on—dogs began to escape their chains and backyard kennels and look for food. Those of us who hadn't disappeared marked the change in circumstance by calling animal control. In the morning, I rushed out to my car before the dogs noticed me.

A blue van playing "Pop Goes the Weasel" drove through the abandoned suburb. Children didn't rush out to greet it because many of the children were no longer present or if they were, they hid from the packs of dogs.

We were all more afraid than we normally were.

Stage 2: Remission

But those odd events of October seemed to recede. Empty houses sold. New people moved in. The dogs were gradually rounded up and taken away. I'm sure all of those dogs found loving families who wouldn't just disappear in the middle of the night. Things, I'm happy to say, returned to normal. In the evenings I walked my dog and collected her feces from well-groomed yards while watching the blue lights flicker from double-paned windows.

I replaced my mailbox. But I had my old box. I contemplated the faintly-red scuff I found there.

Stage 3: Spread

In December before it snowed, but after the frost, in a night where the moon disappeared, leaving the sky empty except for the slowly crawling fall of jumbo jets aiming at the International Airport, I woke in the middle of the night. I heard an aluminum murmur. I had been waiting for the distinctive sound of my mailbox being crushed.

In the middle of the street, a massive red truck idled under the streetlights. It didn't fit on the street. The truck bed jutted over the curb, flattening ornamental shrubs, stray recycling bins, and mailboxes. Men in black fatigues collected families from the split levels and ushered them out onto the macadam road that was unpleasant to walk on with bare feet. My neighbor, a depressed woman with stringy blond and grey hair, wore a ruby sequined nightie. The individual flecks glittered under the street light. Her husband wore a white t-shirt and plaid boxers. Their sons must have slept naked. They had been rousted from bed and rubbed their eyes and covered their privates with one hand. And then *en masse*, the men in the black fatigues ushered them up the ramp and down a shoot. The entire machine looked like a Humvee edition of a garbage truck. It made sense to me that they would have such a thing.

Before I thought about it, though, I ushered my family, still asleep, into the crawl space under our split-level. My wife had a new regime of sleep medications and so could not object. I wrapped my daughter in my blanket. The dog didn't fit. When the dog woke I could hear the dog rushing through the house looking for us, and then they must have been in the house. They searched the house, and then perhaps because they had quotas to meet, continued down the street.

We climbed back out of the crawl space and brushed the cobwebs and spiders off and went back to sleep.

I woke when it was time for work and before I thought about it I had prepared myself for my workplace. I noticed that all of the mailboxes were crushed on our street. At least, I thought that explained that, and then on the way to work, I called my wife and I asked her, "Do you think it's a good idea to go to work considering what has happened?"

"Where's the dog?" she asked.

"I don't know."

"She must have escaped," she said, "When you went to work."

"I think something has happened," I said. "I think something bad has happened."

"We need to find the dog."

"She'll turn up," I said. But the dog was a beagle.

We had picked the dog up at the pound because what happens is a beagle begins to smell something and then follows it to its logical conclusion; everything except their sense of smell shuts down and then they are a sense of smell following a smell. "Besides, we put a chip in her," I said. "They can just do a search on her chip."

My wife still sounded worried. "I hope she's okay."

"I hope so too," I said. And I hung up.

Although I left for work late, the traffic was fine. There was hardly anyone on Interstate-Five. I parked in a free lot. It was pretty much empty; I wondered if it was a holiday. And then when I arrived at the building, the place was empty. It was just a sea of cubicles with dark computer monitors. The lights came on automatically, and so the place was in full operation. One of the programmers who often slept under his desk peeked out. "Hey?" he asked. "Is it, like, a Christmas?"

Stage 4: Collapse

From the car, I called my wife. "I'm coming home." "I think you should. Your daughter is really worried about the dog."

"Do you see any neighbors?" I asked.

"I never see any neighbors," she said.

"Don't open the door for anyone. Keep the house locked," I said.

"What?"

"I'll call you when I get there so that you know to let me in."

"What's going on?"

"They took our neighbors," I said. "They took them all."

"I don't understand what is going on," my wife said.

"I was going to take your daughter to the playground to take her mind off the dog."

"Don't go outside," I said. "Don't you remember hiding in the crawlspace last night?"

"Did I tell you I had a dream that we were hiding in the crawlspace?"

When I arrived home, I explained the situation to her. We turned on the news and the TVs were running old movies. Instead of ABC News, there was Christian Slater in *Gleaming the Cube*. Instead of CBS News, there was Humphrey Bogart in *Treasure of the Sierra Madre*, and for current news on CNN, they were running a special on their coverage of the first Gulf War. While we ruminated on the implications of this development—no new TV programming meant a complete collapse of society as we knew it—I realized I was listening to the ticks and groans of the house. The incessant air traffic over our house had stopped. There weren't any planes aimed at the International Airport.

"They took our neighbors," I said. "They took them all. And it is only a matter of time before they take us."

"Who?" My wife asked.

"The people who took our neighbors," I said. It didn't matter who. It mattered only they had done so systematically and completely. In sweeping the kitchen floor, I did so first with the broom to get up the majority of particles. The lip of the dustpan left a line of debris. To finish it off, I vacuumed until I collected every speck. We had to get out of the kitchen.

That afternoon I searched our neighbors' houses and found their AK47s, their disaster-ready cans of gasoline, their jugs of water. At dusk we loaded an oversized Bronco with canned goods and essential equipment. We began to drive. To the south, black helicopters combed the neighborhood from the sky with searchlights. I drove without headlights through the empty streets and finally parked in a greenbelt not far from the house under an overpass and waited through the night half asleep.

Stage 5: Rebirth

I had seen the movies. I had read the books. I had dreamed of this moment, often.

Before dawn, I drove the back roads into the Cascade Mountains. As the sun began to rise, I drove to a logging road, its width blocked by a locked gate. I parked the Bronco down a short spur, and backed into the brush. I lay branches across it until it was hidden. I hid the canned food in a cache that I covered with leaves. Around us, the air was sweet with pine. The peaks around the valley held the first of the season's snow. We walked down the road, through a swamp and finally, late in the day after scrambling over trees and working our way over the fresh snow, we arrived at a miner's cabin hidden in the crook of a valley between two alpine lakes.

We built a fire and the smoke was lost among the gigantic fir trees and drizzle. And we lived there for many, many days waiting for the black helicopters, waiting for the survivalists or resistant soldiers to come down from the ridges. But no one came. Until one night, there was a scratching at our door.

I grabbed the AK47, and then pulled the door open quickly, and in rushed our dog. We occupied a wilderness where before we had occupied an abandoned strip of highway. We drank pure water from the creek bed and ate snow from the pine boughs. The end, I realized, is the beginning for some people.

A Boy, a Cat, and a Lifeboat

Tony

O cean. Not a little ocean, but a vast ocean. The shot can be done with a camera with a weight hung from the helicopter. Is this really how it might be done?

I'm concerned here about the camera disturbing the waves. I want it to be clear that the boat and the boy, have lost their ship because it has sunk without a trace. It is as good as if they had been dropped there in the middle of the ocean from somewhere else completely.

There is the boat, a white speck, a tiny thing, a toy boat, a boat with two shapes in it.

There is a boat with a boy with a peach fuzz mustache, and a tan drinking water out of a gasoline can, and Tony the Tiger of Kellogg fame.

We build brands and make the world a little happier by bringing our best to you each morning.

He is somewhat translucent and pixilated. It becomes clear, quickly, that this is not a commercial because this Tony the Tiger isn't smiling, but has lost some weight, and that you can see his bones through his carefully cheerful and colorful skin.

How do you achieve this translucent effect? It needs to be true translucency rather than a suggested translucency —that is there needs to be the effect that this tiger is made out of Mylar or some kind of see through material rather than merely superimpose the background image over the top of him. The background image needs to pass through the medium that is Tony the Tiger and into the viewer's eye.

This is suggested by the distortion of the light passing through the translucent tiger. The boy and the tiger are getting along as they always do. They are eating seaweed.

How does it taste?

They're Gr-r-Great! But, it is clear as they are eating, from their slowing down, from Tony's prolonged glances at the boy—he would rather be eating something else. The boy, too, can tell, because he would rather be eating something else. "It surely would be good to get my hands on a nice steak right about now, wouldn't it," he says. "A nice juicy piece of meat." The tiger laughs. He can only say one thing (you know—They're Gr-r-great—or laugh, and so he doesn't say his one thing because he would rather keep eating the seaweed than lose the conversation of his friend. They float on the water for a long time. The passage of time is indicated by a time-lapse shot of the boat in the water. The waves speed up and jostle around the boat. The thin clouds sweep overhead, and stars swirl up as the darkness pours over the sky and then it is very dark.

They will not eat each other?

They will *not* eat each other, but will perish like a civilized tiger and boy. The tiger's will begins to break down. In one instance, he sees the boy shaped like a turkey, dripping baked oils, bread and clove stuffing coming out of his butt. When he leans in to eat the boy, the boy begins to shriek. "What are you doing? I am a boy, not a piece of meat!" And the tiger comes to and sees the boy.

It is a dark moment

Now he is going to eat the boy in any case. Saliva drips on the boards of the boat. The translucent tiger is quite hungry. "A boat," the boy says. "A boat." And they see another boat on the horizon. They jump around on the boat. "We are saved," the boy says. He flashes a bit of metal in the sun. They wait. The boat disappears over the horizon, and Tony looks at the boy again. The boy looks at Tony again. Tony has a bib, and a knife and a fork. Just then another boat appears on the same horizon.

It must be a shipping lane or something.

Tony is undeterred this time. He chases the boy around the boat. The boat jostles in the water, one side dipping down very close to letting water into the boat and then the other side dipping up almost to the top. And then finally, this boat has seen them. Tony is about to eat the boy, and the boat is on top of them, a gigantic freighter, and pulls them to safety.

A close call.

A close call, to be sure.

Trunk

A tiger slept under the tarp at the far side of the lifeboat, and the boy wanted to get under the tarp with the tiger because the sun came down on the bright, glittering sea.

The lifeboat floated with the debris of the sunken steamer, shattered wooden doors, life preservers that had failed to preserve any life, wads of paper, and cloth, and other things that managed to float in the roiling blue water. If the boy looked right down into the sea, it was green. He didn't see the tiger, but knew it must still be in the boat because it had been there last night. When the tiger became hungry, the boy knew the tiger would eat him.

The boy plunged into the water. He slipped below the surface, and saw the boat hull as a dark shape between him and the surface of the water. He paddled to the life preserver, dragged that back to the boat, and hung it from one of the oar hooks. He swam back to the other pieces of junk—floating in various orbits from the boat—and when he went out there, he thought the boat might get away from him, and leave him stranded, clinging to a stray box, his legs kicking and frothing in the fathoms of transparent lime-colored water. The boat never left, though. And finally he had all of the junk trailing from the end of the boat. He found a trunk and tied the end of the rope to a handle, and then he climbed into the boat and was relieved to be in the boat, where it was dry and hot.

The tiger had come out from under the tarp. When it saw him, it breathed its breath, an odor like meat left on the counter. It was a ratty, old tiger; the sleekness of the fur had gone out and left the hair in knots, and pills of dirt on the skin. The tiger disappeared under the tarp.

The boy pulled the trunk up into the boat. The boat rocked, and the tiger made an uncomfortable noise and then the trunk came over the edge and into the boat. The boy couldn't open the trunk. He worked at opening the trunk for hours and then finally as it became dusk, he sprawled down on the side of the boat and slept. At night, the tiger moved around the boat. The boy woke once to see the tiger silhouetted against the light of the moon.

The boy woke in the morning, cold, and cramped from sleeping on the boards all night. There was dew on the wood, and he licked the planks clean of moisture. His lips had started to crack. He didn't like sleeping outside because the air settled on his face and made him feel odd. He felt odd, waking up and he looked for the tiger. It must be curled under the tarp.

The boy resumed his work on the locked trunk. He worried the lock with a nail from the boat, turning it, and finally, he didn't even know how long it took, it clicked. He turned it, and it clicked. He turned it and it clicked and then finally when the sun was high above the boat, and there was nothing in the sky except for a faint speck of something white flying near the horizon.

He opened the trunk. The trunk contained a gun, a case of bullets, a bottle of gun oil, an oily cloth, and assorted gun cleaning brushes. The boy took the gun out of the case. It was a light, steel thing warm in the tropical air with the maker's glyph forged into the bottom of the handle and a number along one side. The barrel was octagonal shaped. The boy put the bullet into the casing. He thought he should kill the tiger. He should just shoot the tiger, and then he would be safe. He loaded the gun and the noise it made, the metallic rattle, clattered over the shiny blue waves.

He pulled the tarp away from the tiger. The tiger twitched its whiskers at him, and lifted its mouth. The gums around the tiger's mouth were black and coated with white froth. The tiger didn't make a noise, but opened its mouth to show the dry tongue and let out the stench of its throat.

The thought of the tiger eating the boy became terrible to the boy. Just the thought of those jagged, nicked teeth piercing his skin caused the boy to constrict. He fired a bullet. The bullet passed into the tiger. The bullet passed through the tiger and then passed through the boat and into the sea, leaving behind a dead tiger, and a jagged and cracked board.

The boy jumped down and pressed the tiger up against the side of the hole. This was enough that it stopped the water from rushing into the boat; but blood and seawater filled the bottom of the hull in a trickle. The boy put the life preserver around the middle of his body. Gradually water rushed into the boat until finally the boat and tiger, and the gun sank and then the boat drifted away in the greenish water and was gone. The boy was thirsty and now wouldn't be able to lick the boat clean of dew. The boy drifted in the current among the debris of the sunken ocean liner. When night fell, he didn't know what to do. He waited. He was a dot on the vast, rolling expanse of waves.

Three in a Tub

Rub-A-Dub-Dub
Three s/hes in a tub,
And who do you think they be?
The tiger, the small boy, the hartlot's daughter.

Turn 'em out, knaves all three.
And how do you think they got there?
They all jumped out of a rotten potato,
'Twas enough to make a man stare.

Waterscape with Tiger

I had been pleased, to be sure, to get rid of mummy and daddy and my nursemaid. I am fifteen and too old for nursemaids, surely. I have been indulged, certainly. I am entitled to indulgences but had felt since I was twelve at least that I should earn my indulgences on my own or I would never be a man. My parents had been done in when the SS Hanover, in the middle of the night, caught fire and sank to the bottom of the swell. There are down there among the sand dollars and sea cucumbers.

I think it is clear to the other occupants of the lifeboat—a naughty scullery maid from the kitchen, and a scruffy and arrogant tiger that managed to escape from its cage and board the lifeboat before the liner plunged into the deep. A fire broke out. An optimistic soul let the circus animals from their cages. Giraffes and elephants stamped around on deck and then suddenly, this tiger jumped into the lifeboat and the lifeboat tumbled into the sea. If I hadn't already been in the lifeboat trying to unfasten the maid's dress attempting to earn my own indulgences, I would be with my mummy among the crabs and sea anemonies.

I don't know her name, and now I'm not sure if I want to ask because the tiger has been purring and smoking his paw-rolled cigarettes. He isn't very good at rolling them since he lacks an opposable thumb. They begin to come apart after a few seconds. Bits of burning tobacco fall on his sleek fur and singe it. "Your coat is beautiful," I tell the old boy. "It is really stunning. You belong in a cage if you are going to damage it yourself that way with that filthy habit." The tiger didn't enjoy the chastisement. It is well known that smoking is an awful habit. He just glanced at me and wagged his whiskers. He didn't say anything. "In all good time," he seemed to be saying. Perhaps he even said this, but it is well-known animals only talk in children's imagination.

He was a splendid tiger. The most beautiful animal I have ever seen up close. He didn't look this way surrounded by the scratched and beaten trappings of the Asian Pavilion King of the Circus Rail Show. He sat there at the back of his cage, lethargic, and would growl meekly at passersby. But now, under the glittering Indian Ocean sun, a few puffy white clouds for contrast, his fur filled the horizon with an orange cast. He turned and dove into the water.

The scullery maid jumped up, and then slapped me. "He is my tiger," she said. "I helped him on board the boat. He is mine. Don't say anything else to him, unless you get my permission."

When she slapped me, her dress was still untied from the night before, flapped open and I could see her bra, gray and threadbare, but a woman's bra nonetheless; I wanted to broach the subject, since it had been dropped so suddenly last night. I wanted the maid, yes, but, I also I wanted the tiger.

We could see the tiger below us doing the crawl. He was deep underwater.

When he finally climbed back onto the boat, he had three fish. He handed one to me. He handed one to the maid—she had told me her name, but the name of a scullery maid, why would this be important to me last night? Now it was of course, but she assumed I would care enough then to remember her name now. Before the SS Hanover went down we lived in a different world. I would like to reassert that aspect of the old world that provide me with my entitlements. I would like to say to the tiger, get back in your cage where I can look at you. I would like to say to the maid, get on your back where

I can get at you. I could do these things before. And I wondered now at the power I had, and how, now that I didn't have them that this attitude cost me. It cost me dearly. Because the girl was now pressed up against the side of the tiger and the tiger shared his fish with her and she shared her fish with him.

I ate my raw fish, alone, on my side of the boat. My fish tasted like seawater, but I was hungry and bit through the slick silver skin and ate the meat to the bone and then threw the bone into the sea. Something snapped it up before it hit the water.

The girl fashioned a divider out of a piece of the tarp that had covered the lifeboat. It was kind of a tent, and she and the tiger went inside the tent, leaving me to sit outside under the searing sun to contemplate a drink of water.

While I sat there, I saw that we were drifting toward some specks on the horizon and then gradually the specks began to grow in size. I wasn't sure what they were. At dusk, the girl and the tiger came out of the tent. We sat on the edge of the boat at dusk. When the sea finally became dark around us and the stars were above us, we partied. The tiger had a recorder, and I played drums on the side of the boat and we played songs and sang until late at night. We stayed up until early the next morning and watched the sun come up slowly. Out on the sea it was not light, and then it was a faint light and then gradually more light, and then finally the sun came out of the ocean and began to climb into the sky. We all slept under the tarp again, to keep out of the sun. I had my own space.

I woke before they did. They slept for a long time or just kept to themselves under their portion of the tent. I smelled the tobacco smoke. The dots on the horizon had grown, and I could see now they were islands with trees and we were headed toward them. They grew, and

I watched them gradually get larger, and at dusk, I could see around them a kind of whitish fog that I knew was the surf.

We spent the night partying as we did the day before. At dawn, we passed a rock. It was rock sticking up out of the ocean with barnacles on the side, and at the very top a cap of moss and a single, withered, bush with berries on it. The boat skirted the stone by about two yards, close enough we could see the veins in the leaves and the hairs on the berries.

Ahead of us, we saw the islands with mountains and all around it the wild spray of the sea rushing up onto the beaches in huge waves. "We will be swamped," I said.

"Better than being on the sea," the maid said, and I agreed with her, but still a sudden watery death didn't seem preferable to a life of midnight singing and raw fish.

We guided the boat as best we could toward the largest island. The boat began to pitch up and down on the waves, and I said, "Maybe we should figure out another way to go in," and then finally, the maid said, "Directly to shore. Cats hate water, you know."

The waves picked us up and dropped the boat. We were then down inside the waves and around us the water towered above us, and then we were way above the waves, just a tiny sliver of the boat in the water, and then the wall of water behind us slid up and crashed down, forcing the boat forward, where it stopped and then dragged back out to sea and then the waves did it again. We did this a dozen times, each time I thought that was it. We were still hundreds of yards from the land and would get swamped by the waves, and then the boat shot forward and passed much closer to the shore but still the trees on the shore were tiny. And then, a wave came down, and slammed into the boat and we were in water and bubbles and air and then the boat was still in the water half underwater. We were now much closer to the shore. I could see the scales on the palm trees now and the individual leaves and the coconuts, and then, finally, a gigantic wave crashed down on us and we were not only underwater, I was being dragged across the sandy bottom of the water. My mouth filled with salty sand, and I couldn't breathe sand or water. When I could again move I was underwater, a frothy mix of bubbles and green water and then I found a pocket of air and I spit out the sand and breathed in, and then I stood up on shaking legs, I was on the shore.

The boat capsized in the surf hundreds of feet out into the water. The girl fell face up on the sand a half mile down the beach.

I ran to get her and when I found her, I found that the tiger had eaten part of her. In any case, she was missing a portion of her collarbone, her arm, and spleen. I saw tiger tracks on the beach. I surmised what had happened. Perhaps she had drowned beforehand?

I followed the tiger tracks, and they led across the beach and into the forest where I lost them and then looked into the dark bushes. I wondered what I was thinking following the tiger into the bushes like this? I went back out to the beach and crabs had already come out of the surf and had pulled out the girl's eyeballs. Two crabs fought over one eye and then divided it and scurried back into the sea. I found a part of the shattered lifeboat and dug a pit for her. Late in the dusk, I rested her in the pit and started to cry because I was alone, now. Well there was the tiger, and I wanted to see the tiger again, but nonetheless I wanted to escape the island.

The surf came across the vast expanse of ocean where they'd come and hit the island and broke up. The waves were tall. In the darkness, I went back into the forest and found a dry place to lie. I woke many hours later to see the tiger sitting in the surf. The tiger got up and began to walk around, and then finally it stood on the loose mound of sand where I'd buried the girl and it sniffed there and then it looked into the forest where were I was and I remained completely still.

The tiger stood up, sniffing, and came toward the bushes and then stopped and hurried away.

A figure walked along the beach then. A man with a long, lanky beard. He picked up the pieces of the boat, and he leaned down and looked at the place where the tiger had been and then he stood still for a long time and finally came over to the bushes and looked down. I remained still, and then the man pulled me out of the bushes and onto the beach.

He said something that I did not understand, and then he looked around at the beach. He said something again. And then, I realized he was asking me a question, but it was a very mumbley question.

The man had a canteen and gave me water to drink, and I drank the water. I wanted to drink all of the water, but the man stopped me.

The man took me up into the forest to a hut. And in the hut, he fed me fish, and a baked carrot, and I ate until I wanted to be sick.

In the morning, the man showed me a pool of water where I could swim and bath. There was soap the man had made out of ash and oil. We washed and once we were clean—I had not thought about his nakedness—the man grabbed me and while he had me, I wished the tiger had eaten me instead of the girl and then it occurred to me that this would have happened to the girl as well. When it was done, the man cried. His tears fell on his body. He patted me on the head and then walked away, leaving me at the hut, near the waterfall that came down from the mountainside. I drank some more water, since I'd earned it.

The Boy and the Wild Cat Went to Sea

The boy and the wild cat went to sea
In a beautiful pea-green boat.

They took some honey, and plenty of money,
Wrapped in a five-pound note.

The boy looked up to the stars above,
And sang to a small guitar,

"O Lovely Pussy! O Pussy, my love,
What a beautiful Pussy you are,

You are.
You are!

What a beautiful Pussy you are!"

Tiger in a Lifeboat™

The main problem was that the tiger would either eat the child in the first half-hour of the show, or the tiger would act like a big house cat until it starved to death. The desired effect of the show was that the cat would behave like a house cat with the inevitable, intended promise that it would eventually, freak out and eat the boy. The boy through cunning and guile had to survive—not that the boy would survive because he had bonded with the cat. This was the problem they had uncovered after going through several hundred test boys—that is boys without any clear identifying information that they had bought from the homes on the streets of LA. Four hundred bucks could buy a functional seven-year or eight-year old. They preferred English speakers, but many of the boys spoke Spanish. One boy spoke a haunted babble they could not identify but thought might be Linear Pict X. Thirty of the boys died within minutes of getting launched in the test lot with the tiger.

They tested five tigers—and this became a problem, too, because the tigers that learned to kill continued to kill (and got better at executing the boys) and so the producers learned that once a tiger did the kill, it would keep killing. And this became part of their thought process in putting the boys in the boat with the tiger. They would have to have a supply of tigers, as well.

Of course, all of the boys had to die because no one could know how they had perfected the show. It had a lot of problems, this show. It was a delicate balance to get it to work.

Yann Martel had to be contacted and he threatened to sue if they went ahead with the show. The public domain idea, he said, was a boy and a wild cat. A boy and a tiger in a lifeboat, I have that copyrighted. If you do this, my lawyers will contact you. So they paid him a half-million dollars for the rights and threatened to say they would call it *Yann Martel's Tiger in a Lifeboat*, playing both to his ego (like anyone even knew who this guy was) and his pretension, what kind of literary guy was he if he'd originated a reality cable show?

Reality was played out anyway. This was a latch ditch effort to get some interest behind the show. Early one morning in a warehouse in Burbank, they launched the boy and the tiger in the lifeboat, and waited.

The Ribbit-Powered Float

On quiet summer afternoons before my father left for work at the kitchen where he was a cook, the house filled with the odor of incense and the buzzing of a stray housefly or two. Dad spent long afternoons puttering in his greenhouse, filled with orchids, rare ferns, a tank with terrapin turtles, and the sound of hundreds of tiny frogs. The moist air and pools of water attracted the frogs from the forest. After he finished work in his greenhouse, my father stretched out on the mossy stone behind our house to stare at the sky.

We lived on a glacial moraine of bunched up clay and massive stones left by a receding glacier thousands of years ago. The activity of these glaciers was still evident in our neighborhood. Walking through the forest we would find huge stones that had been rubbed smooth by the ice. The stone behind our house was one of these rounded monoliths. It was flat on the top, and a bed of moss rimmed with tiny ferns grew over it.

My father talked about his flying dream. He didn't want to fly in an airplane, but he wanted his body to sail in the air just above the top of the trees. "This is the big dream, isn't it?" he said, "to just float."

He took me to the skating rink. From outside the rink was a cinderblock barracks. When we paid we could hear the throbbing disco from inside, the distant grind of wheels on the polished wood floor. This was an era before in-line skates. Everyone wore roller-skates. They wore fussy old men shoes attached to a metal plate with huge rubber wheels. Practiced skaters floated just above the surface of the hard and polished floor, scuffed with the marks where people who had lost it. My father could skate as well as a swallow could fly. We would rent our skates, and then he would strap his on. He leaned over to tighten my shoes. "You'll get it," he said. To the sound of the brothers Gibb—a music my father normally avoided—he zipped under the disco ball and seemed to hover.

We came infrequently enough I never learned any degree of comfort with the skates. I struggled out onto the floor, keeping to the margins, so I wouldn't slow anyone down. I clung to the shag carpet walls placed helpfully for neophytes like me. Eventually after struggling around the rink two or three times in the dark, I began to experiment with leaving the wall and rolling. I kept my body bent down, and then a foot would start to move forward and leave the other one in place. I pin wheeled to keep myself up. I tried to roll and then my feet kept going and left my body behind, and I slammed into the ground. Just as I started to gain a degree of confidence, couples skating or fast skate would come onto the board. I would have to make my way to the benches under the rattling glow of the video game machines. During couples skating my father would sit with me. During fast skate, my father would race around the track.

He took me to a field once to practice cartwheels. He said he once saw a man who could cartwheel for miles. He just rolled and rolled and rolled like someone had taken him and hurled him across the ground.

We practiced on the damp grass, planting our hands in the long grass and then found our bodies curled and heavy above us where we collapsed. Finally after sweating and getting grass stains my knees, I managed to do a single cartwheel. Frustrated my father found a grassy hill and we rolled down it.

My father's favorite song was by the Beatle's, "Flying" from the *Magical Mystery Tour* LP. We went to see Superman the Movie on the opening weekend because my father wanted to see him flying. My father liked the movie but didn't like the fly. "How does he fly? If he was just incredibly strong, he would really be jumping. But, he flies—defying gravity and somehow able to generate not only propulsion but the ability to navigate? Does he have rudders in his boots?"

"It's just a story, Dad," I said.

"But it is flying," my father said. "Everyone wants to jump into the air and fly. This is why everyone loves Superman. He can fly."

"There are airplanes," I said. "There are gliders."

"But the machine is flying," Dad said. "You are just along for the ride. Wings and an engine do the work."

He talked about the lighter-than-air flying machines constructed in the early days of air flight. We talked about balloons filled with lighter than air gasses. He said there are substances that are lighter than air. "You'd think air would be the lightest thing," he told me once, "but there are things in the world even lighter than air. And then, there is something they don't even know what it is yet, but they will know what it is one day, anti-gravity. When they get anti-gravity that will solve all our energy problems."

I didn't know we had energy problems. Our only problem was a well that ran dry in the middle of the warm summers. For a month, the world would suddenly ripen into perfection. No school. I could take long trips to the library and read books and find the ones I wanted to take home and on the way home I stopped at the store to buy an ice cream. And then, when I got back home, the entire forest around the house still held the cool morning air. My father sprawled in his spot, inert, on the mossy stone staring at the blue sky contemplating flight. I took my book and found a quiet place alone in the forest.

When our well ran dry, we took baths at a neighbor's house closer to town. They lived next to a vast strawberry field on a plot of land thick with cedar trees. The strawberry field, muddy in the spring, was now a vast flat field of baked earth. Huge cracks opened in the ground. Our neighbor's house was green like an oasis. We took baths and then filled gigantic, square jugs with water. Taking a load of water home one evening, my father had an idea. "I could fill these with lighter-than-air gas," he said.

He built a body suit that he would fill with a lighter-than-air gas, and then he would be able to fly. "I'll just soar into the sky," he said.

He began to research gas. He found he could create hydrogen by passing a current through water and separating the single oxygen atom from the two hydrogen atoms. After constructing an elaborate mechanism he managed to fill a jug with hydrogen. But, he was unhappy with the result. The hydrogen could barely lift the balloon. He was afraid, too, of repeating the Hindenburg, which had been a hydrogen blimp. He imagined himself falling out of the sky on fire.

He learned, though, that cows produced methane. He

began to talk about hooking up a pipe to the cows in the field next-door and filling sacks full of methane. The farmer wouldn't let him. Lying on his rock dreaming the next afternoon, my father thought about the frogs that filled his greenhouse. He would use them to fill his bags. Frogs produced methane, too, only it wouldn't smell. "I will create," he told me, "a ribbit powered float."

He captured the frogs and hooked straws and tiny bags to their bodies. For a week the frogs hopped around and then one morning, the frogs all floated to the ceiling attached to tiny lighter than air bags. My father removed the bags, tied them off and stuffed the bags into his suit. Within a month, his suite was floating on the ceiling.

In the morning, he drank his coffee. He walked out into the already warm air. The sky was a blue dome over us. He patted me on my head, and then put on his suit. He didn't ask me to fly with him, and even if he had, I didn't want to intrude. He strapped it on, and then my father was floating like a balloon. "I'm almost flying," he said. "Untie me."

I untied the length of rope. He floated above the trees. He was laughing and crying. "This is flight!" He soared into the blue sky.

Trestle

My uncle Ezra used to take me into the woods to fish for trout. We made arrangements during the week when Ezra came over to eat. He drank a beer with dinner. My parents didn't drink anything, ever, even if we were at one of the occasional parties at the house of my father's partners house where the old lawyers would drink, a lot. On Saturday Ezra arrived and parked in the driveway, idling, until I could sense he was there. I didn't hear him. He didn't knock or honk or anything. I went out into the cool dawn. The air smelled like the lawn, and the greenbelt across the street. Ezra sat in the driver's seat reading the paper and drinking coffee from the cap of his thermos. The steam rose in a column out the window. He didn't say anything. I climbed into the car and clicked fast the heavy buckle. The truck smelled of metal and oil and the ripped seats that lost hunks of yellow foam.

We drove for an hour at ten miles over the speed limit toward the mountains. At first we passed along huge cement walls built to keep the freeway noise out of the developments. Ivy grew on the wall, and in some places graffiti had been covered with grey or white blocks of paint. Then we passed through the countryside full of cow fields. I couldn't tell what they used the field for. Finally we parked on a gravel road. The City of Seattle had posted signs: *No Trespass*. On one side of the sign it was woods, and on the other side of the sign it was woods. But because they had posted these signs, I imagined that it was better woods on the other side of the signs than it was on my side. There must be something interesting on their side. It seemed likely that if they went to the trouble of posting signs they would have some way of making sure people didn't just scoff at the signs. I looked into the forest. It was just ferns and fir trees and a bed of moss.

"It's the watershed," my uncle said. "We can keep going. The signs keep everyone out, so there is no one to stop us."

"We will contaminate the water supply," I said.

"You think the deer read the sings?" he said.

"Deer are natural," I said.

"Shit," Ezra said. As an uncle, he could swear around me. My mom would give it to him if he said what he said when she was around, but he still said it. So, she gave it to him sometimes. "Bear shit is natural, but that doesn't mean you should drink it."

He kept walking down the track. There was no one out there, just the trees moving in the wind that blew down from the snow filled valleys in the mountains. I watched my uncle walk. I waited for him to turn around or something but he kept moving and then he was gone. He was my uncle. He could leave me in the forest to die. He didn't have to look after me. My mom was his sister. He'd been losing and breaking her stuff since the day she was born.

I found the forest remarkably spooky. Unlike the trees in the greenbelt near my house, filled with dirt bike trails, spots where losers had dumped their trash, ant hills, power lines, the gravel road along the pipeline where the middle schoolers gathered to drink wine coolers and smoke, this place was empty. There were cattails with their fuzzy tips, tiny lily pads floating on the black and silver ditch water, and the tracks rubbed to a bright line by the passage of the lumber trains. The rest of the tracks were rusted brown.

The trees had been growing for decades before I was born. They would be growing decades after I was dead. In the greenbelt, they were surrounded by the cul-de-sacs, edged by preschools, kindergarten, and middle schools. There were office parks and bowling alleys and retirement communities and a vast cemetery on the hill over the lake where Bruce Lee was buried. In just thinking about the landscape where I lived, I understood what would happen to me and my remains. The trees in the watershed moved in a gust of ice chilled air. I ran down the tracks careful to keep my feet landing on each tie so I wouldn't trip and face plant on the gravel or the rail. I tried to stop thinking about Bruce Lee's headstone littered with the junk people left for him. No one ever gave the dead anything expensive, at least not since the Egyptians and the invention of plastic.

I followed my uncle for miles. I expected the watershed police to step out of the forest and handcuff us or to come riding on reindeer and wearing bright orange Gortex raincoats. I wanted to get off the tracks where it seemed likely we would be caught. The rail went over a trestle and my uncle stepped in the bushes and disappeared. When I tried to follow him, I found it was just mud and roots and was like climbing a ladder right down into the earth. At the bottom after we stepped through the salmon berries and devil's club we stood on the gravel banks of a huge pond. The trestle crossed over one end. At the base of the pilings, old logs, sticks, and bark had accumulated into a dam. At the other end of the pond, the stream ran through the wood jumping through cataracts and tumbling down a waterfall. The black stone was slick near the waterfall and then coated in a thick carpet of moss. No one would find us here. We fished until we had our trout and then my uncle took out beers and we drank the cans sitting in the dim light of the culvert.

Maybe it was the illicit beer, but I loved coming to this secret place that was both beautiful and completely forgotten by the people who had built the massive trestle. One time a sound came from the distance, a kind of screeching rumble like an avalanche flying over the trees, and then an engine pulling a row of cars loaded with raw tree rounds, the branches freshly sheared off, the bark lacerated from the clear cut, passed over the trestle. In the canyon with its stone sides and already the nearly deafening roar of the rapids that fed the pool the air itself began to shake and rumble. When the train passed the sound remained in my ears and it wasn't until we were in the car and driving back out down the gravel road that my ears popped and I could hear again.

I didn't even know where this place was that my uncle took me. My uncle got cancer and maybe even already had it when he was taking me there. While he was sick no one in the family wanted to know about it. They didn't say anything about him until he died and then they all pretended they missed him but if they weren't visiting him while he was sick, how much could they miss him? It wasn't like they could catch it or anything. I feel bad I never went to see him, but removed from the context of our fishing trip I never had anything to say to him and when I thought about seeing him I thought better of the awkward silence that would surely greet us after I saw him. Death is something that the dying have to deal with and the only way they comes to terms with it, is to die. The living don't know what it is; if they did, they'd be dead.

Blue Glass

I wake one night and the worm has come into my room. Its decanter shaped head hangs down in front of the window while the rest of the transparent blue body coils around the ceiling top. Organelles float in its milky interior. It pushes out on the walls of my house. Its pale segments pulse, and drip clear fluid. I feel hot specks spray my arms and legs as my headache flares up, and I tumble out of the bed and the worm drops from the ceiling like a wet towel. It rolls me across the floor with its broad, six-sided head. I hurry into the bathroom and pour cold water over the back of my skull. The water washes into my ears and plasters down the short hairs on my neck. All I can think for the longest time is about the wash of cold water in my ears and the throb of my head and when I look up I see that the twitch from my stroke has returned. The skin all around my left eye constricts like a frozen wink.

I think of the pain as a worm because one night it was so bad I couldn't even concentrate enough to practice my relaxation method. I took a deep breath, and another deep breath, and dust ran over my lips and into my stomach until my belly throbbed with musty air. I even tried to imagine lying under a tree in the summer, and I had all day to lie looking up at the leaves spiraling in the riverside wind. And then, I tried to draw my headache with pen and paper thinking maybe if I could see it, then I could do something about it, because the physicians, and the physician's assistants who are not nurses, and the nurses who are not physician's assistants couldn't do anything. So, I drew a long, hard nightcrawler with skin like the cobalt glass decanter my wife, Lana, broke the day she went to the hospital.

I often wake in the middle of the night with this pain. I sit up on my side of the bed and breathe in and out the way I learned to do at my physical therapy class. The hospital took CAT scans and blood tests and said, "Mr. Kirche, we can't detect anything but we can recommend another couple of options." The fact that they couldn't find anything confirmed my worst suspicion, that the young people were incompetent and the last good doctors; the ones my father's age had died a long time ago. It also indicated that the kind of wear and tear of the years which eventually kills a person had finally set in on me.

I went to the classes they recommended. One of them was for loonies, real nut cases. One guy believed a bread-toaster had been transplanted into his brain. They all took themselves very seriously, straight men to the last one. We sat around in a circle on hard plastic chairs that inflamed my prostate so much I couldn't sit for the rest of the day. By the time it came to be my turn to spill my guts out like a bucket under a leaking roof, my headache sounded so pathetic I told the group a lie. I said this to make myself comfortable and because I have always been one to fit in. I told them I believed it was the end of the millennium. The instructor said, "It *is* the end of the millennium." "Well," I said, "I believe that it is the real end of the millennium and that time will completely stop after I am dead. It will stop for everyone. That'll be it. Also, I have really bad headaches that wake me up in the middle of the night..."

I learned the breathing; Lamaze I think they call it. Managed care is too cheap to solve my problem. Instead, they gave me this course where friendly young instructors teach holistic health for unbearable agony. It doesn't help much, but it gives me something to do when I am about to vomit from the electric pulses of pain that constrict the capillaries in my temple. I wish they'd burst. It would serve them right if I suffered an aneurysm right there on one of those wood and fabric monstrosities they pass off as furniture in their perpetual waiting rooms. I am bitter about death. I am not a product, like one of these new Coca-Colas that needs to expire. I have kept on living even after my wife Lana gave in and died. Even though the statistics speak in her favor, I am still alive. She had plans and strategies to keep herself going. She read her women's magazines and kept current on all the latest breakthroughs in longevity while I ate donuts and steaks. We even sometimes talked about it. "What are you going to do after I am dead and gone?" And she said, "Honey, it's none of your business."

Every time I said, "You're driving me crazy," Lana would always say "Short drive."

I miss her. I often wake with the worm tangled around my forehead in the middle of the night, and then I rise and stare over the cattle field next door. The cows stand along the fence between my place and the young guy's house next door. The herd has a whole field, even with a pruned cedar tree out in the middle of it, but every night the cows crowd up to the electrical fence and talk to themselves, a constant groan and bellow that drives me insane. Their black hooves churn the ground and the earth makes a deep throated pop as they raise and lower their legs. This could be the cause of my migraine. Or maybe the cattle line up to watch the show as this blue worm squeezes the life out of me.

Tonight, a car idles out on the road's wide gravel shoulder. The ditch edge, like the slope of a deep tub, drops suddenly into the roiling runoff. The car lights die, and I let the drapes fall back. I sit on my wife's old makeup table and wait until the car door opens. When it does, the interior light flickers, and I see the boy, a tall, skinny kid with the beginning of a beard and an earring. I suppose the earring is just the beginning, too. The girl wears a long white dress and a dark sports jacket. She jumps over the ditch like a ballerina and turns around against the barbwire fence as she twirls her entire body. A heavy gust rushes down from Steven's Pass and bounces against the air flowing in from the Sound. Rain splatters over my bedroom window and I watch her spin, and then she climbs onto the rotting fence post. The wind whips her dress as she jumps out into the field. The end of her dress brushes the wire and snags the barbs and rips as she lands. I hear her yelp, "Damn." She twirls around again to show the boy in the car she's fine, and then she races across the field to the gate. The yard lights flash. Her father, Mr. Sand, stands under the cattle light. He grabs his daughter by her arms and shakes her, just like the tough man handling a moll in one of the old movies. Her head shakes, and then he leads her inside and I can hear his voice followed a second later by her crying.

I have some old records that my wife's father used to own back in Chicago. I don't know where he found them. A couple of them feature a lone guy, and a guitar, and he's playing and he wants to find a gambling woman, he says; and I listen to that record of that guy singing this and I wonder what he means. Does he mean a wild, loose woman? A whore or a woman who lives like a man? I like the records, but I'm not exactly sure what they're talking about. And looking at this girl coming home in the middle of the night I'd do just as her father is doing, waiting up for her and I'd make sure she didn't leave again. But, if I were her, as well, I'd sneak out every chance I found. And if I were this boy, I'd do what he's doing, which is passing back and forth and throwing the spent cigarettes into the ditch.

So, I'm stuck between two competing points of view the way I always am. It kills me that Lana's dead, but it's also a thrill, because I won. I know what the world is like without her and she won't ever know that. She knew what it was like before me, but she'll never know what it is like after me. I can assure everyone, it will be a much degraded place. But it'll probably get better mileage on account of all the depression and weight I throw into the backseat; still, it won't be as good.

It's a strange fact about our neighborhood. Some noises carry for a long way. I swear in the middle of the summer I can hear people hollering from the top of the mountain. The wind must catch their voices and whip the sound way down the mountain like a piece of paper. And then on the same days I'll be strolling by the river with my fishing pole and not hear someone crying in the cedars up on the river bank thirty yards away; I'll not hear them until I'm right on them. The noises that carry over from my neighbor's would make a good daytime TV show. The things I hear aren't always favorable. Sometimes I can hear their TV, and sometimes I can hear their music, strange discordant slashes of sound. Just the other day I heard Mr. Sand yelling at his girl. It's none of my business, and I don't know what he was yelling at her about, but it didn't sound any good. But, what can an old man like me do? I made my choice a long time ago not to get involved with the people who live around me. I've been old for a long time. The nice thing about being old is that I'm not young, because when I was young I had this fear of just being old and having survived a life unlived. I wanted to fit in as much living as possible. Looking back, now, so much of the time I spent could hardly be classified as "Living with a capital L." I've ended up with a life of false starts and derailed plans. I think of the summers trapped on my father's farm in Carnation as the best times and it was those summers when I wanted to leave the most. I'd wake up in the middle of the night with cold sweat trickling down around my ears and shakes in my rib cage, and I was anxious to get started. Started on what, I don't know. But damn, I wanted to get started, now. I felt I was wasting away in nowhere Washington State while the rest of the world was hopping and humming with jazz and wars and living with a capital L.

The farm manager, on old man who called himself a coot and had bright white dentures, used to laugh at me when I'd talk about the world I was missing. We sat on the porch drinking beer brewed in the back shed, and he chuckled. "It isn't going nowhere. When you go out there you won't have missed anything." He'd been in the Spanish War and had driven cattle across Texas, and I thought he was just talking through the side of his mouth because he'd done everything in his day and the fact he was still drawing air and able to drink a beer now and then was enough for someone who had done everything. I hadn't done a goddamn thing. I wanted to go out into the world and to do something even though I didn't have the vaguest notion of what I meant. And no matter what this old man said to me, he wasn't going to calm me down.

My neighbor, Mr. Sand, he's a middle-aged man who wants to be a farmer even though he's spent most of his working life working at car lots in the new neighborhoods around Seattle. Four years ago, I met him when he moved in stuff, big pressboard bookcases from some new furniture store and several loads of small, sleek, and black electrical appliances that looked more like fancy luggage or cases to power tools than things in and of themselves. He saw me weeding my garden. Don't get any ideas about me hunched out there in my pea patch pulling out weeds by the handful. I can barely lift the hoe these days. I'm an Ortho man. I spray everything and let the magic of industrial pesticides, and the fertilizer seep into my soil. I stood, weeding my garden, so he must have thought I was just watching him, which maybe I was, and he said to me, "You live here?"

"For now," I said.

And he didn't like the sound of that and scowled and looked at my patch with the tomato plants I never can get to do anything and the zucchini that I can never can keep under control, and he finally smiled. "That's some garden."

"This is the land for it," I said.

"Do you own all this?" He waved his hand over my house and the field that I did own all the way back to the forested belt next to the river and then the house next door, and the field across the road. "I'm going to be farming out here," he said.

"Yeah?"

"Cows and chickens and goats. You name it." And that's when he told me about his plans. He said his name was Vern Sand, and he had plans to have the biggest farm and bed and breakfast in the valley. "Well, good luck to you," I said. And I watched as he placed cattle in the fields around my house, and I even rented him the lot behind my house. I liked the cows suddenly being there, and I'd talk to them sometimes when I went out to get my mail.

I could hear Vern at two o'clock in the morning yelling at his daughter, and I heard doors slam and then a window shattered and I heard someone crying. I admit I was listening for something. I sat on the edge of my wife's old makeup table, and the window was open and I could smell the rain coming down through the cedar trees. Sometimes that night, I didn't hear anything except the cattle at the fence and the water running in the ditch and then the wind shifted and I could hear Vern yell. I suppose it's all the yelling that brought the worm around anyway.

That girl over there, she'll be old. But, her father is still young and he won't ever be old. He might get gray hair and a big gut. He'll dye his hair even darker than it was when he started in the first place. Even now, he sometimes drinks whiskey and gets in his pick up truck and turns around and around in the field, throwing mud way into the air.

I wake the next morning with my headache unwinding and falling to the floor. Even though the sky is overcast, a painful glare fills the room and I close the blinds and shuffle into the bathroom to take a glass of water and a handful of aspirin. I walk out and sit down on the edge of my bed with the growing conviction that I will dust. Perhaps the particles in the air are responsible for my headache. After I shower I put on an old cardigan and corduroys and open all the windows in the house until cool fresh air flows through the whole place. I read somewhere that ninety percent of the dust in a house is human skin. Human skin is an organ, like my liver or heart. I want to get rid of the remnants of myself and my wife, and all the people who've lived in this house.

I dust with my wife's old slip. She'd stained it during one of her last menstruations almost twenty years ago and I'd washed it and set the stain. I remember her tossing it onto the stair banister while she folded the laundry.

"Thanks for your help," she said. "At least there'll be no shortage of rags."

She used one of the cloths cut from the slip to polish the oak dining room table. One time I'd set a coffee cup on the surface of the table and Lana ran across the room and pulled up the cup. She placed her hand down flat on the table as though she was a preacher laying on hands. Her fingers kneaded the surface and she'd stared at me while she did that. "You did this on purpose," she said.

"What? What did I do?"

"Twenty years of wax applied in smooth, even patches, ruined."

"I did not intend to do it."

That Saturday she sanded the surface with sheets of sandpaper. She removed the wax until the table sat half-stripped The raw wood filled the dining room with a wholesome sawdust smell. It smelled the same as the woodpile behind my own great-grandfather's house filled with the cords of wood from a great oak split by lightning.

Later that Saturday, I had a stroke while walking to town. I paused on the walk under the grove of cedar trees by the mailbox. The road crew had cut the tree so often that it grew up in five main trunks and then mushroomed out under the telephone wires. The fragrant boughs shed orange needles all year, and old branches and needles littered the asphalt. I don't know what happened exactly except that I felt this sudden constriction at the base of my head, and I lay in the spongy pile of needles and couldn't move. I sat there for a long while; I know because the light changed and finally a car stopped and someone I didn't know stood over me. All I could see were their knees and ankles and unlaced shoes.

I came home from the hospital and sat in the living room for a long time not able to move. I don't remember sitting there at all, now, but Lana told me about it.

"I'd feed you at eleven and then again at five. You seemed real happy with that schedule." As quickly as it had happened I could move again. I lifted my hand and Lana leaned forward and kissed me. I don't know how long I had been like that. During that time, I remember sitting in a chair and Lana feeding me out of little jars. She'd sit next to me while the TV played, and I'd watch her as she noticed whatever was going on there, blinking and then grinning and cheering at a game show.

When I started to get better Lana told me that while I was in my stroke she found she had cancer. "They say I've had it for quite a while." She started to get worse right away, and then we were driving into Seattle to go to the hospital, where they gave her the radiation and she lost her hair and wore a bright red wig like Lucille Ball.

The day we bought the wig we decided not to go to her chemical therapy class. We decided this on the drive into the city and so we stopped at Borracianni's Bakery on Empire Way, what's now called Martin Luther King Way, and ate three Danishes each. We hurried out of the car on account of the rain. It was raining so hard that it practically flattened Lana's new wig; I stood under the awning, watching her look at herself in the dark window and she turned around and said, "Everyone knows it's a wig, anyways." And we bought our Danishes and went back out to the car and watched the rain roll and roll down the windshield, and I liked that because the coffee smelled burnt and the Danishes were warm and she didn't have that wig on anymore.

The table never was finished because as she got worse

and even angry, she sat on the couch reading the books she'd bought over the years but hadn't finished. She had stacks of them on the couch. "You didn't finish them to begin with," I said, "because you didn't like them."

"I always told myself I'd finish every book I started. It's disrespectful to the author."

"They're dead," I said but when I started to say it, I wanted to stop myself but my lips already moved, the sound had already spilled out and she threw her book at me, a heavy translation of Nikolai Gogol's *Dead Souls,* and it kicked me in the shoulder and hit the base of the cabinet where she kept her blue glass. A six sided decanter from the top shelf tottered and shattered on the floor next to the book.

"I'm sorry," I said, and sat down on her pile of books and held her and she shrank down from under me, letting me hold her, but then I thought what was she going to do? She couldn't go anywhere no matter how mad she got at me.

I kept getting better, and she continued to get worse and finally she told me one evening before we went to bed that she couldn't do it anymore. "Each minute I'm afraid the pains are going to get worse," she said. "And it does. It just keeps getting worse."

"I love you," I said.

And she said she loved me and we were lying in bed, and she was sitting up doing crossword puzzles and then she turned off her light and lay next to me. I put my hand on her shoulder blade. I didn't want to fall asleep. I tried to stay awake and listen to her ragged breathing but somewhere along the line I did fall asleep. Death is slow. I often wished while driving Lana to the hospital that we would just live and live, and then one day be gone without any of this stuttering and shuffling toward our final minute. I wanted to die like an old TV set, just blink and shrink out of existence and be gone.

While I'm sleeping I'm aware of all the life around me, the sounds of the cattle and the comings and goings and of the Sands girl. While I slept Lana died next to me and when I woke she'd left, and I hadn't even realized I needed to say, "See you later."

After I dust that morning I put on my jacket and walk from the house, down the road to the bridge where Joe Stremick used to have a dairy. I walk across the cow fields to the blackberries growing in the shade of the fir and poplars on the swampy river edge. I walk into the old cut up to the base of the mountain. I know the trail through the berries into the forest where the ferns grow. Each fern holds a knotted mass of previous seasons' fronds and sticks, and rotting leaves. The virgin stumps come up out of the forest. I like this path through the recovered second growth forest, not old enough to be of interest to anyone. Nonetheless, it has returned to wilderness. I walk though the trees brushing the strong anchors of wood-spiders and stop to listen to the distant knock of a woodpecker and the thrash of a chipmunk in the underbrush. A forest, even as worked over as this one, has a steady, quiet life.

I find a small white flower that grows for two weeks in the early spring, long before the rest of the forest starts to jump under the flowing sap and warm spring fogs. I carefully lower myself down and remove my glove and pinch the flower stalk. I smell the flower. It doesn't smell like anything beside the stalk, and the water caught in the petals.

"What are you doing? My dad says you can't pick wild flowers. It kills the roots and they'll never grow in that spot again."

I stand and almost fall down again as the blood rushes to my head, and then I worry that'll start a headache and the worm will unfurl from the branches. I find Vern's daughter standing on the hill above me. The girl wears a long black coat and a black beret and the fine strands of her hair jump from under the hat and down her shoulders in wild convolutions like water spraying past a thumb-blocked garden hose.

"Here," I say and hand the flower over to her.

"I don't want your murder victim." She laughs and carefully steps down the hill. She takes the flower out of my hand and brushes the tip of her nose with it. "It doesn't smell like anything."

I want to tell her something about myself. To warn her about hanging out with boys or to tell her about her father, about how bad it is now, but it will be good for a long time after that. But, she won't listen or care about the ramblings of an old man. So I just stand and make several inarticulate stammers.

"Aren't I a little young for you, gramps?"

She runs away. She waves her arms in front of her to catch the spiderwebs away from her face. Sticks snap under her boots like dry bones. I stare through the trees after her, listening to her movement, a murderously loud sound after the quiet taps of woodpeckers and the twirl of birds, and then she is gone into the gloom under the fir and alder.

Years ago, when my eyesight began to fail, everything gradually fell into the shadows. I could still see, but the sense of things became less obvious to me. For instance, when I met someone in a room, I focused on their face but the detail in the rest of the space—the cups on a table, the pictures on the wall—these things faded, and I began to assume everything had always been so narrow and focused. I could still see and hear, but things began to pass unnoticed into the shadows. I try to follow the Sands girl's steady disappearance into the woods. I want to catch her and let her know. "Know what?" I wonder.

I stop when I think that. I look around and think there isn't anything to tell her that she doesn't already know. I keep following her, walking of course, and at the top of the incline where the logging road cuts across the slope, I find the flower on a mossy stump top. The petals are already limp, as slack as the white silk collars of one of my wife's old blouses.

The Cemetery Dogs

Kayla took her terriers to the Crown Hill Cemetery early on weekday mornings when the only living things stirring were the blades of grass. The place had plenty of space for her dogs to run, roll, and work out their boxed in dog energy. They spent maybe too much time in her condo locked in their kennels where she put them when she got sick of them climbing onto her lap or getting snippy and nipping her. From the moment she removed them and strung their leashes onto the master, and herded them into the back of the Pathfinder, they twitched and panted.

When Kayla sold her stock options, the SUV seemed to be not just an extravagance but the first in a series of extravagances afforded to her by her ballooning wealth. She had thought coming out of college and starting work that this was why people worked—wasn't it?—to earn money. Lots of money. She worked a lot of hours;

it followed she deserved a lot of money. When the tide of stock splits receded, and then fell below their IPO to startlingly low levels, Kayla was glad she'd paid cash for her condo and SUV; at least she had this, she thought. She considered selling her stock, her place, her car, and finding a laid-back job, but where then would she put her dogs?

Kayla's mother who'd worked thirty-five years as an executive secretary always said she was as close "as broads in my day could get to CEO." Kayla disliked her mother saying *broad* or bringing up how soft life had been made for her because of her mother's suffering. Her mother didn't know how hard it was. Her mother didn't understand Kayla's money or even what she did to earn it. Her mother asked, "If you don't go to church, then how can you be a technological evangelist?" Her mother was undeterred by Kayla's sudden poverty, or rather, loss of money since Kayla still earned a plush income by her mother or the rest of the world's standards. Kayla's mother regarded financial set backs as a necessary condition of life, like gravity or friction. "If we didn't want what we couldn't get," she said, "We would have no reason to do anything at all." The implication, Kayla felt, was that she had just been given what so many people wanted. Her mother didn't understand: first, Kayla deserved what she had been given because she had received very good grades in school; second, suffering only made people bitter and cynical. Hadn't Kayla worked the hours required by her managers to clear one project deadline after the next? She had, hadn't she, cleared her schedule of the late night drinks with her college friends at the Cloud Room, the weekends out of town to attend their weddings, and the spare change of their early evening and afternoon showers, newborn displays, birthdays, and various recitals? Hadn't Kayla taken the complete obliteration of her assets, more money she might point out than her mother had made in her entire thirty-five years sitting in front of the CEO's office, in stride? So, she wanted what she already had, this was a good thing. She had a new car with a global positioning system that could tell her exactly where she was stuck in traffic and a luggage compartment full of purebred wirehair terriers with a minimum of genetic problems.

And anyway, she had bought the SUV for good a reason. She didn't have enough room to take her dogs to the park in the used Corolla that her mother had bought her for college. When she walked, she spent almost the entire evening walking to the cemetery and back to the house. She had to tape Friends and watch it after ER. She much preferred watching it as it was broadcast when everyone else was also watching it. When she walked, too, her dogs worked at wrapping the chord of the leash around her legs, tripping her on the shoulder, and dragging her, bouncing, down the middle of the street. She took the terriers to the cemetery, because once, when she had taken them to Green Lake, the dogs had chased an old woman into the shrubs where the dogs kept her until this jogging Samaritan stopped to remove his headphones to use as a whip to drive her terriers back from the overly dramatic old woman. At the cemetery there weren't any fragile old people or any children to object when Kayla's dogs finally broke loose and chased down a squirrel. They never caught the squirrels but that once when Kayla took them to Ravenna and a toddler started to cry because the dogs actually cornered one. Children should be taught, Kayla thought, to look away from acts of nature. Kayla's head dog, Valerie, caught the poor animal by the tail and flung it into the air. The other dogs ran. The little girl screamed herself hoarse when the squirrel came apart like a broken string puppet. At the Crown Hill Cemetery, though, Kayla didn't have to worry about the opinion of little girls and fussy old women. Her dogs could just run.

Valerie, Maryanne, Cisco, Lawton, and Hanna scratched at the door when Kayla turned down the gravel road into the cemetery. They yipped and barked and fought each other for the position directly in front of the door. "Calm down," Kayla said. "Calm down or we aren't going to take our morning walkies." But that only worked them up further. Whenever she took tone with them, Kayla had observed, that only made them worse.

"Keep calm, gals," Kayla said. She called them all gals even though there were two male dogs. Valerie was the head dog despite the fact she was sterilized, or maybe because she was sterilized. Valerie had once been sweet and docile until she had started suddenly to lose weight. Kayla took her to the vet. She had uterine cancer. They took out her uterus and something else; some kind of maternal quality, and the new Valerie resembled the old Valerie but vibrated with a nervous hum. When Valerie returned from the vet, she quickly established herself as the alpha male, pulling out Cisco's fur.

Kayla opened the Pathfinder door. Valerie plopped out first onto the grassy margin between the road and the graves. The other dogs scrambled out after Valerie had circled the car. Kayla noticed that the headstones only somewhat conformed to neat rows and that really they sort of wobbled back and forth over the plot lines. A man rolled a stroller through the far end of the cemetery. Normally no one came to the cemetery in the morning.

Kayla had taken her dogs to shows. Valerie of course couldn't go anymore. She had gained weight after the operation and her fur had turned funny, spotty, like Astroturf in a few patches and long and curly in others. Lawton had a nervous condition and chewed on his butt until it was nude and raw. She tried Beethoven, Mozart, and Handel. She played music from her Soothing Classics collection of CDs to find something to calm Lawton down, but nothing Kayla played did anything except stop Lawton from thrashing around and gnawing on his open sores.

A half-dozen crows took off from the ground as the terriers raced over through the graves. The birds' sharp voices echoed against the maples, cedars, and crumbling mausoleums. Kayla's dogs ran through the cemetery, knocking over a flowerpot, tossing up freshly distributed grave dirt, urinating on lichen-encrusted headstones. Kayla went over to set the pot straight.

The man pushing the stroller looked up at the screaming crows and said something to his baby. "It's all right. They're just barking about something. That's how dogs talk." The man had come closer and Kayla could see he needed a shave and a shower. His hair stood up in thick cowlicks. He wore a faded blue t-shirt. "The Copper Gate. 50 years!" Kayla vaguely recognized this as the name of a fish and chips stand, maybe, as something local but neither tourist friendly nor scenic.

The baby sat up in the stroller. The baby pointed at the crows. They baby cooed, a noise Kayla could hardly hear from across the cemetery. The baby had soft white hair and a thick, bulbous nose. Kayla thought the baby looked ugly. It could be the distance. It could be a bad morning for the baby. She had often thought of her dogs as babies and when she thought this, she thought how she had never really seen an ugly dog. Her babies weren't ugly. This baby though looked deformed maybe. Poor man.

Her dogs then noticed the man and the stroller and the ugly baby. "Come. Come here, gals."

This just set them running. A cloud of dust flew and hung in the air. The pack circled the stroller.

The man said, "Look at the doggies."

The ugly baby made a guttural, very poor imitation of her terriers' bark.

"Go away doggies," the man said.

Valerie started to howl and that was the cue for the other dogs to start to bark and they all barked and darted back and forth toward the man and the stroller.

The man leaned down and picked up some stones.

Kayla's dogs had never had anyone throw a stone at them before. His gesture didn't even slow them down. They kept coming. "Hey," Kayla yelled but she thought in all of the noise, of the man shouting and the dogs barking, that her dogs or the man couldn't hear her.

The man threw his handful of rocks at Valerie. They bounced off her head. Valerie became very confused and very excited by the man throwing rocks at her. Kayla started to yell. The man couldn't hear her she realized because he hollered in a thick phlegmy voice. "Get away! Go home doggies!" He threw handfuls of gravel at her dogs. They yipped as the stones rained down. Valerie ran past him. And then the other four dogs jumped on the man.

"You're getting them excited!" Kayla shouted. "Don't get them excited. Just let them burn off steam."

The man continued to holler. He leaned out into the path of the pack and kicked Cisco up into the air. Cisco flew several yards, yelped, and rolled. Hanna and Lawton climbed up onto the man's legs, and then dug into his back. Valerie had made it to the man's stroller. "What have you done?" Kayla yelled as she started to run across the park.

The baby's cry and howl filled the cemetery. With three snarling terriers clinging to him, the man grabbed Valerie by her back. Valerie wrapped around and started to swallow the man's elbow. The man threw Valerie to the ground. He dropped on top of her in a single World

Wresting Federation knee slam, a maneuver Kayla felt he had seen on TV and practiced drunk off his ass in his backyard with his other car-on-blocks neighbors. The man's knee scattered the gravel. When he stood up, Valerie didn't run away. The other dogs circled the spilled stroller. The baby still howled. The man flung Hanna and Lawton off his back. They ran away and then all of the dogs except Valerie ran back to the Pathfinder.

Kayla hurried after them. She fumbled with her keys. She turned on the car alarm. She turned off the car alarm. She unlocked the doors. She locked the doors. She unlocked them again and let her dogs into the back.

She knew Valerie wasn't all right, which didn't immediately make her think of the quickest routes to the vet but instead suggested to her the following image: a handsome man in a shiny button-down shirt and grey wool slacks sat at her dining room table, talking and drinking chamomile tea from one of the floral English tea cups her mother had given her. The dogs' water dish rested upright against the recycling bin filled with tensile, crumbs, stray hairs, and other floor sweepings. As the man spoke, he leaned across the table and lay his fingers on Kayla's forearm. But before Kayla could really let the implications of this thought sink in, Kayla knew than that Valerie wasn't only wounded, but in all likelihood, mortally hurt.

The man righted the stroller. He leaned down to examine his hideous child.

Kayla couldn't hear anything. She didn't know what to do. Her impulse was to leave as soon as she had the dogs in the Pathfinder. But she had to see if Valerie could be rescued.

The man had made her dogs excited. No one had thrown rocks at them before. What would she do if someone threw stones at her? Kayla would defend herself to the death. The only natural thing to do. Self-defense. That was the phrase.

The man began to wheel the stroller toward her, briskly.

She started the Pathfinder and then watched him in the side mirror, wheel up to the car.

"Yes?"

"You left your dog back there."

"Is your baby all right?"

"Do you have a cell phone?"

Kayla did. She had a cell phone.

"Can you call the police?" he asked her.

She wasn't going to call the police.

"Can you call the police and an ambulance?"

Kayla saw that the man bled from a gouge in his shoulder. A dark stain spread under his blue t-shirt. Three holes punctured the skin exposed by the shredded fabric. Blood came out, a thin, black rivulet. He grabbed her cell phone from the dash and dialed 911.

His baby sat in the stroller and looked at her. A pink bonnet rested askew on her nearly bald scalp. She sucked her fingers. It really was a very unpleasant looking child. Kayla had wandered into a very bad place. This baby with its pale skin, its little flowery frock, it's snout of a nose, and the man with his unwashed face, his ripped t-shirt, and coffee stains on his shorts had ambushed her and her dogs. The baby had a gash just over one eye that traveled down the side of her head and ended at the chin.

"Is your baby all right?"

"My baby is alive," the man said. "Not all right. But your dogs will be destroyed."

Kayla stumbled out of the Pathfinder. The man smelled like sweat and liquor. She locked the car with her key chain.

The man thrust something at her and Kayla jumped

away from him. He wagged the cell phone at her.

He wheeled the stroller away and sat down at a bench. Flowers wilted in the vase on the marble headstone. The wind had stripped some of the petals from the flowers, and the thin slips of blue and white and orange rested on the grass. Over the grave, a godseye swung from a thin alder branch.

The Mall

The day after I received my orders for the war, I drove to The Mall. I parked in the outer limits of the parking lot and walked through the vast, empty stalls under the endlessly tall light posts that stretched into the low cloud cover. When I opened The Mall door, holding the large, hinge-like handle, the warm mall interior puffed out into the damp day. I could smell the perfume counter, leather, and suede, the faint odor of disinfectant.

The girl I knew who was currently my girlfriend stood in the middle of her store folding and refolding sweaters. I watched her and didn't want to disturb her work. She turned and looked out into The Mall, but I don't think she saw people out there—just a gauge of traffic, assessing how busy the day might be.

I waited on the island in the middle of The Mall. Thick jungle vegetation, rubber plants, palms, gigantic ferns grew up toward the skylight in the middle of The Mall. A man in a motorized wheelchair rolled past me. He waved one arm randomly in front of him as he if he were parting the air. He stopped in the middle of the wide space where two wings of The Mall intersected. Normally, when there were crowds in The Mall, the people milled toward the food court and the two main department stores, JC Penney's, The Bon, and Nordstrom's, positioned for their draw so that they would force circulation through the entire mall. He went into the Squire Shoppe on the corner. My girl finally noticed me sitting out in the middle of The Mall. She gestured at me, and I couldn't tell whether she wanted me to go away or to come into the store. I just looked away down The Mall.

Finally, she came out, and sat on the bench next to me. "What time do you have to go to work?" I should tell her about the war. We hadn't talked about it. She didn't even want to know about the Army Reserves. I felt like I was drafted, but I wasn't. I said I'd go if they asked and they'd asked.

"Two hours."

"Don't you normally go home after class?"

"I go running on Thursdays," I said. "I run hills."

"Yeah. You have something to do. Always training those muscles."

"Today I came to see you. It's nice to see you." She wore a black blazer and a pale tailored skirt and black tights and her worn work shoes. She smelled like citrus, not an organ or lemon, but something with a rind.

"What's wrong?"

"Nothing."

"You don't just come by and see me. You were going to pick me up tonight after work, right?"

"Yes."

"I have to go back to work." She stood up and brushed her skirt down over her legs. She leaned down and kissed me on the lips and then stood back away from me fairly quickly and looked around The Mall to see whether anyone had seen her, and then she looked back at me and smiled this sort of relieved smile, a big smile I guess. She never said to me, "Where do you see this going?" She didn't know where she wanted things to go. We had never had those kind of talks.

The man in the wheelchair came out of the Squire Shop with a bag in his lap.

My girl lived in The Mall. Only twelve-year olds or immature thirteen year-old girls loved The Mall, but everyone who lived in the hills above The Mall had to go to The Mall to get their school clothes at least, to get gifts for their mothers on Mother's Day, to buy their toasters, cheese graters, and new pants. Well, soft boys—any punk who spent all day watching TV, playing video games, and making special trips to buy Charleston Chew's at the 7-11—loved The Mall. I'd been a soft boy at thirteen. I remember the smell of heated popcorn oil back when they popped the corn in coconut oil. I remember the warm rubber trees standing in lush, narrow jungles in the planters in the middle of The Mall under the skylights. The distant ceiling arced somewhere above the pedestrians, lost in the tumbling light, the scattered track lights, the trailing banners decorated with the heraldry of universal advertisements that might have been placed during some past epoch, *Peace on Earth, Tranquility, Love your Neighbor.* The light in The Mall was merely an intensification of the diffused outdoor light that passed through the filter of clouds, a refinement rather than a replacement of the outside light passing through the hazy, dripping clouds hugging close enough that the tops of tall fir trees and street lamps disappeared into their diaphanous margins.

As a thirteen-year-old boy, I welcomed The Mall as a

place to find refuge. I was a soft boy. I lift weights now. I entered The Mall with the vague music playing somewhere, recognizable tunes strained through an electronic colander to mingle unrelated pop styles into a uniform buzz. "Mack the Knife," "Fever," or "Twist and Shout" became aural equivalent of the slab floor that never seemed to wear no matter how many millions of strolling teenagers migrated across the floor from the teens section on the kid floor of JC Penney's to the row of fleeting stores along the margin of The Mall. The clothing style changed--somewhat new colors and slight alterations in the basic idea of dresses, blue jeans, blouses, and polo shirts. The record albums changed--somewhat new formats in the basic idea of ten song recordings with the faces of musicians on the cover. But, the Muzak adhered as strictly to the catalog of songs and sound as the gold veins in the marble floor flagstones and the pebbles in the white pillars in the central hall. Mall facilities erected beauty pageant stages in front of audience bleachers and radio station promotional cars festooned with call numbers.

My girl started work at Lerner's as soon as she turned sixteen. She started to earn money for clothes so that she wouldn't have to bring her parents along when she bought outfits. She received a store discount. Even so, her father worked at The Mall at a stationary store that had been in The Mall since it opened. The store along with the tailor, office supply store, and grocery store belonged to an older conception of The Mall as small town Main Street. Her father wore a suit and metal-rimmed glasses. He sometimes drank coffee with my girl at the French pastry shop, which was the first store to spread its tables out into The Mall like a sidewalk café.

In the month I started to date my girl, The Mall ripped out the decades old planters in two periphery hallways. They began to remove the old rubber plants, ferns, and palms, the simulated stream with its wishing ponds. They placed brick down the middle of The Mall and leased the space to kiosks, carts, and digital accessory dealers with glass cases. The merchants sold Tupperware; drawings of Jimi Hendrix; wooden lawn objects, butterflies, deer, a grandma bending over to weed in her garden with her butt sticking in the air. They sold nothing I would deliberately buy; however, while killing time waiting for my girl to end her shift I wandered through the busy space. It had transformed The Mall from a sedate, Novocain-infused clean space able to absorb even the Christmas crowds in its wide marble halls, into a hectic street fair. Customers and stray people who had just happened to become stuck in their orbit surrounded each kiosk.

In its transformation it began to attract people who came to The Mall as a place to go. It needed things to sell people who had no intention of buying anything. But, it also had the older stores, like the department stores that still attracted the old style customer who had just come to The Mall to buy something. My girl knew everyone in The Mall, especially the worn women who sold makeup and clothes. She was even on speaking terms with the spinsters at the B. Dalton's—a crew of woman in stirrup pants and cardigans with squiggly black facial hair capping scabrous moles. They sometime tried to lure her into the store with talk about the latest article in *People* magazine. When my girl passed the store they followed us down to the edge of the Penny's hallway and stopped. "See you later," they would say and return to their stations in the store, one at the register, and one near the men's magazines.

She knew the wives of gangsters. They were bored and friendly with the service at all of the places they shopped because they had plenty of money to spare and could only trust the congenial attention of people they spent money on. One woman took my girl for coffee after she bought her week's clothes. She would not wear any article of clothing more than once, and so she had the task of finding a new wardrobe every week. "Even her underwear," my girl said. "She just throws those away. The rest of the clothes she gives to her friends."

My girl operated as a perfect child of The Mall, even though she didn't drive a car herself, or rather because she didn't drive a car herself, she existed in relationship to the other people and The Mall. Her father gave her a ride as he headed to work. When I finished my lunch shift, I would pick her up. The Mall originally operated on clearly defined parameters and was built to take care of its operators, but in the late eighties it started to change, and the pretense that the place was an indoor town, the illusion that it was somewhere else, ended. Instead, it had become The Mall, an end in itself with customers who came to The Mall because it was The Mall, not because they wanted to shop, necessarily—and it sold expensive coffee drinks, carefully set price points of disposable junk that people would buy because they had come to this commercial space and felt obligated to leave with something even if it was something they didn't really want or need—a plastic egg stuffed with M&Ms, a scarf, the new Madonna album. The employees could no longer park near the entrances with their dented Datsuns and scratched Ford Escorts. They had to park beyond the perimeter, out where the blackberries had started to rip up the asphalt, where the standing mud puddles were so old they developed schools of fish and cattails grew at their margins. At night, they hiked the half-mile out behind the parking lot sodium lamps into the region of spotty lights where some lamps fluttered and others had been out for years. Deep mud puddles were rimmed with the flotsam of cigarette butts and Styrofoam to-go shells. Jackrabbits, their fur matted down with parking lot runoff, jumped into the blackberries. A girl from The Limited had been raped on the way to her truck. An older woman from The Bon had disappeared. Her Prelude sat out there for a week and then was gone. At first, the employees tried to establish a parking lot in a well patrolled, well-lit periphery of The Mall. Everyone did their jobs, and the parking had worked in the old days, but The Mall was under duress itself. Market forces had changed, and strip malls had grown around The Mall attracted by the consumers attracted to The Mall. The way The Mall had eaten the downtown city near it—Renton—the strip—South Center Parkway—was eating The Mall. The Mall said it could do nothing about employees who didn't obey commonsense safety tips. It issued a tri-fold explanation of walking safely to your car, and left it at that. Every evening, the closers at my girl's store walked in a group out to one car and then drove around to the other cars until everyone was safely in their cars and could leave The Mall.

My girl wore perfect make up. She had long black hair, and skin as white as hand lotion, as white as anything engineered and sealed in form-fitting plastic. Her lips were as red as an impact resistant joystick throttle. She wore clothes of the season made out of up-to-date fabric. Her favorite author was Truman Capote. Her favorite artist (and she meant it and understood the irony) was Andy Warhol. She owned more than several tapes by Madonna. She was interested in fame not as a form of escape, wish fulfillment, or escape from Mall life. She was interested in celebrities the way some people are interested in Feudal Japan, Dog Breeds, or species of rhododendron. A decade of reading *People* magazine gave her a command over the arcane of pop facts. She could name Waylon Jennings' third wife and the two kids they had together. She could tell the story of Madonna's first video shoot. She knew the concert dates of Depeche Mode's *Music For the Masses* tour.

The Mall did not command this information. The Mall didn't have a history. Its function was to dispense and expel, not to collect, and archive. For her to have recall over this information in turn gave her a sense of control over The Mall.

Beyond the projection of mass culture, the display of its brand names on backlight Mylar panels, behind all of these things, The Mall was just a massive brick and concrete box. It was crumbled around the edges. The foundation had cracked. Dropping my girl off early on a Sunday morning in the empty parking lot and entering the silent hallways, I could see the old cornfield the place had been built on, the shoddy and hasty construction of the vast space that had to be filled with noise (such as music), and odor (such as perfume), and carefully calibrated crowds in order to function. Otherwise, it looked like a provisional grain warehouse.

I walked across the parking lot toward my car. I just wanted to get in and drive to a place where the Military Police wouldn't find me and send me to the war. I didn't even know anything about the war, and I didn't want to know anything about it. They had teased me at work. I had just grinned, even though I couldn't really stand them teasing me about being in the Army Reserves, because I didn't want to be thought of as an army guy. And yet I belonged to the Army.

I walked past my car over the broken pavement through the strip mall to the Green River that ran under the office parks. I sat down on a damp bench, even though it got my back wet. There was no way to get out of it. I had said I would go and I would. A gaggle of geese grazed in the grass on the bank. They sent a scout up to the bench. The heavy goose had a thick black neck and grey feathers with a long, greenish tail feather trailing behind it. It stood in front of me, leaning forward and honked. I sat forward on the bench and it scooted back. The other geese turned away from me. I stood and walked between them. They jumped and hopped away. I slid down the bank and stood against a half submerged stone with river water riling against one edge. I thought about just throwing myself in, not to drown, but to just float away down the Green River to where it turned into the Duwamish and I would sink below the murky water and lose myself in the heavy metal river bottom sludge.

Curry Masters of Baltimore

The restaurant owner liked both the cook and the waiter equally and with that balance, he managed to keep the tension in his restaurant turned toward well-cooked food and solid service. But several things kept his business from flourishing. The restaurant suffered from a certain ethnic authority. Indians enjoyed his food but were uncomfortable with the prices and the location of the restaurant near a private school without many Indian students. Also the waiter and cook despised each other. When the waiter came in from the street in his Members Only jacket, he waited until the cook went back into the storeroom before he grabbed his lunch and then sat at the far end of the restaurant. The waiter told the owner that the cook couldn't read. "Not that good teachers didn't try," he said, "but some people are so close to animals. They call it dyslexia, but that just means their brains are more like those of dogs. Some people are very close. It is well known that even the best teachers cannot teach a dog to read." When the cook arrived at the restaurant early to prepare the food he filled the kitchen with music he was certain would shred the waiter's delicate ears. The cook drove a motorbike, a dented green Honda. He carried the key to the restaurant in among keys to all of the apartments and houses where he'd lived in Baltimore. He kept the long jangling chain fastened to his belt. He listened to tapes of the bands he followed and stopped sometimes to listen again and then clucked and shook his head. "Some people should not do that," he would say. Punk Rock was his life. Most mornings he had time to spare between getting ready the ovens and cutting up the vegetables. He went into the alley behind the building with a cup of tea and smoked and read *The Sun*. When the waiter dragged in his attitude, the cook didn't want to hear it.

The cook told the owner that he couldn't trust someone like the waiter because the waiter was always talking behind someone's back. In confidence, the cook said, you shouldn't trust a man like that.

The owner, a young Indian man, had moved to America to get away from his parents. His only other relatives in the entire continent lived in Vancouver BC. He didn't see them. His life in India had been a series of family obligations and working in the family factory.

For months after his arrival he'd been busy setting up the restaurant, finding a place for it, interviewing staff, buying furniture, and learning how to work in the United States and what steps he needed to do to make sure his business succeeded. He had a dream of lines piling up around the block to visit to his restaurant, but when in the first week they had a dozen customers, he thought he had a made a grave mistake. But that dozen grew to over a hundred the second week, and during the days thereafter they had enough business. The weekends were more sedate unless something big was going on campus. He went over to the campus and found a schedule and posted it over his desk. Now, the restaurant closed early in the day on the first half of the week and left him with the afternoon and evening to walk the streets of Baltimore and think about the possibilities of his new life in America. He found in Baltimore hidden parks and green belts and a tea shop under an apartment building that used the same kind of urn the tea shop he used to frequent while he was in school in India. He sat beside the river with his cup of tea under a flowering cherry tree, and although he felt free, he also felt of no real consequence in the world. If some crazy person stopped to shoot him in the head, he might not be missed for several days and eventually his mother would receive the news in India. How did they send news of someone's death now? He'd always thought they sent a telegram, but the idea that a telegram would arrive to inform his mother of his death seemed unlikely. Perhaps some municipal official would call and then tell his mother. Her reaction was beyond doubt though. She would blink back her tears and say, "I told him not to go," and his life and more, his absence, would boil down to an anecdote about his mother's wisdom.

He didn't know how to use his new freedom and it occurred to him one day after he had his tea and realized he'd gained some weight because sitting down on the wall by the river required him to bend in an awkward way before he settled down that he needed to find a passion. Eating scones with raspberry jam and drinking tea hardly constituted a passion. Free people pursued their passions. He'd sometimes fancied that he could write books or imaged himself playing an acoustic blues guitar like the great Delta musician Son House. Learning to play an instrument seemed too daunting, and he already knew how to write sentences and had written several stories in school. Usually he thought he could write a book when he was reading a novel and suddenly he became aware of how it was written. His desire came mostly from wanting to write books unlike the books that inspired him to write in the first place. He picked up the catalogue of evening classes at the university and enrolled in a class, "Ten Weeks to a Best Selling Mystery Novel!"

He sat in the back of the class and took notes and at one point they had to write a scene where someone discovered a body. Everyone then read their scene out loud. With every student, the restaurant owner thought he could have done that. He wiggled in his seat when he read his piece and glanced up thinking that his classmates must have been thinking the same thing, they could have done that.

After class, as he walked back to his house, one of the classmates said to him, "You're work slaps me in the ass." She was a middle-aged woman with dyed black hair cut in a pageboy. She carried her papers in a black velvet satchel.

"Excuse me?" He recalled her scene, a woodshed killing with blood bloated termites.

"You're work slaps me in the ass."

"I don't follow you."

"I like what you read, it means that at least." They stood next to a hedge under a street lamp. Its sodium light cast sharp shadows under the hedge but made everything else dark—the field beyond the hedge disappeared into the gloom and reappeared way down below at the sidewalk next to the street bordering the campus. She looked at him and her purple lips flushed toward him as she cocked her head. He didn't know what she wanted.

"Thank you," he said, but that wasn't it. She just blinked at him. The mascara clotted at the base of her eyelashes. "I have to go," he said.

"Look forward to you seeing you at the next class."

He thought perhaps he'd been wrong about his passion and called the night class offices and persuaded them to let him change his enrollment to "Learn to Sing Your Blues Away." While he carried the guitar for his class to his apartment, the owner briefly imagined people mistaking him for a musician. He passed people on the street and gave them a grave nod. He arrived at class with his rental guitar and promptly broke his string. He also learned how simple the blues were to play. The songs shifted from a mysterious noise into a simple schematic laid naked and simple and as monotonous to him as a clock.

The owner was having a difficult time meeting like minds in Baltimore.

The waiter, however, knew Indians and knew the owner of the restaurant had come from a family with a great deal of status in India. The waiter talked to the owner about world events and literature and they spent an occasional afternoon in the empty restaurant. They both wanted to write books but both of them didn't really know how to go about it and it took them a long time to get to the point where they could show each other their attempts at writing books. The waiter finally asked the owner outright, "Can I see the manuscript you are working on?" And the owner said, "Only if I can read yours at the same time." Both of them went home and opened the drawer where they had their skimpy piles of pages in no shape to show someone else. Both of them imagined the other one pulling out a manuscript, crisply typed cleanly copied, brilliantly written.

The next night, they didn't mention anything and this not mentioning anything stopped their conversation and although they both wanted to show the other one their work because they had used the word *manuscript* because they had talked *novels* rather than *short stories* because they had talked *novellas* rather than *sketch*, they were afraid to do so. They were afraid then to even bring up the topic of books least the other one ask to see their manuscript.

The cook however listened to music. After he heard the owner had enrolled in a guitar class, he said, "I don't know how it is India, but in America, the written language is dead. Everything is written in sound now. I write songs, myself. I would invite you to come out and hear me perform them but I suspect the crowd might be too rough for you. You might like it and then maybe you won't."

The cook had for a long time kindled a hope of making a living making music or at least as a recording artist rather than purely the player in a bar band. He knew musicians who worked very hard to sound like other musicians who had just released records. They never got a company interested in them. However the cook maintained hope that one day after he had spent years doggedly pursing his career as a musician and stuck to his musical principals that someone who could make things happen would take an interest in him. In the meantime, he played his guitar. He played, now, in a punk band that was mostly old metal heads whose deteriorating condition prohibited them from playing the speed metal they truly loved and were relegated to the much slower punk mode. The front man couldn't scream anymore. He could howl for hours and he dressed just like a late seventies punk with a Mohawk and safety pins holding his ripped clothes together. He wore the whole nine yards. He would cut a thin slice into the base of his scalp and howl and parody all the usual roster of easy to mimic has-beens, Mick Jagger, James Brown, Axel Rose and then parody himself parodying them. He attracted quite a crowd.

The owner went to see the cook play with his band. He drank beer at the back of the bar. He felt more and more gone. He listened carefully but the music seemed intent on offending him. Carefully listening he realized the music was not made for listening but made for talking over or talking under or for slamming yourself up against other people or for the skinhead who smiled at him from across the crowded room and made his way over to the owner and sat down next to him. He said something to the owner.

"What?"

"I said, 'Blackie, swim back to whatever country you fucked out of.' " He said this in a bad British accent. He pulled a stiletto out of a sheath in his long black boots.

The restaurant owner didn't know what to do and said, "Nice weather we're having this spring."

"What?"

"Nice weather?"

The crowd oscillated and the guitar playing cook noticed the skinhead and he stopped playing and the whole band jumbled around the abrupt end to the music. The front man continued to gyrate, oblivious to the fact the music had stopped.

The cook said, "Who's that in the corner with a knife?" This is not cool, man."

Instead of scaring the skinhead, the skinhead now had an audience of punks. He stood up and he flashed the knife and stuck it up to the handle into the owner of the Indian restaurant's thigh. At the sight of blood, the punks started hitting each other and body fluid and torn clothes started to fly. After several minutes of breaking glass and howling and the meaty thunks of bodies falling onto the dance floor, the peel of sirens filled the streets and alleys around the club. The owner of the Indian restaurant ended up in the hospital and had the knife removed and put into a plastic bag. They released him with a pair of crutches and a limp.

The cook felt bad and they didn't talk about the incident nor did he ever ask the owner if he liked his guitar playing.

The owner didn't talk to his waiter or cook about anything beside the order of business after these two incidents. Because they were sorry about what had happened between them and their employer, they worked very hard and tolerated their differences and no longer saw themselves vying for his friendship. The owner changed the recipes to agree with how the people in Baltimore thought Indian food should taste. He worked on the recipes until they matched exactly the critics' idea of a good Indian dish, no matter that he couldn't eat now in his own restaurant. No matter that the waiter stopped arriving early to eat. No matter that the cook always prepared his meals separately. But it didn't matter because the cook and the waiter brought to their labors the concentration of the guilty and the business picked up. Food critics brought to the restaurant by rumors of incredible food, raved. Slowly the restaurant began to win more reviews and more customers and the owner hired another cook and more waiters. Every evening the lobby filled with customers waiting for tables.

The cook left first and then the waiter but by this time it didn't matter to the owner of the restaurant because everyone who worked there felt obligated to justify their presence in such a thriving, profitable business.

Caffeinism

A Jones for a Cup

Harris Reilly's mother worked in a dime store in the neighborhood where he grew up. His father worked for a delivery company until they let him go for his nervous twitching and sudden outbursts. After a long day driving on the slick streets of Seattle in a truck with bald tires, Harris' father burst into the foreman's office and yelled about how the company's miserly attitude about maintaining the trucks was going to cost them a lot of money, money in insurance claims from wrecks caused by the bald tires, money from merchants who lost goods in overturned trucks, money from maimed truckers. Mr. Reilly had been drinking cold black coffee from a square fruit jar all day. The cab of his truck smelled like stale, spilled coffee. His teeth held the dark yellow gloss of thirty years of caffeine. He drank so much coffee by the end of every day, he staggered up the stairs into the apartment and didn't move, except for his twitching eyelids.

After the foreman fired Mr. Reilly, he spent a lot of time in the apartment. As a child in the morning, Harris had to be very quiet because his father slept on the living room couch. His mother woke and dressed. She pulled her hair back because she had stopped using the blow dryer; it woke Mr. Reilly. He often slept under his clothes, using them as blankets, having taken them off in the middle of the night because they were too constricting and lying naked in front of the open window had made him too cold. As a result of this way of life, he caught a chill that wouldn't go away. The capillaries in his nose burst. He carried around a handkerchief, and slowly his father's sniffling defined the presence of Mr. Reilly more than even the oily smell of perspired caffeine. When he finally woke, he rinsed himself off in the bathroom and neatly oiled and arranged his hair, Mr. Reilly stood in the kitchen chewing aspirin while he waited for the coffee to brew. He washed the powder down with the first cup of scalding black joe. Until the aspirin and coffee pacified his trembling hands, he kept his cracked red eyes under his tangled eyebrows fixed on the dripping coffee. If someone made a noise, he would turn away and he might break something, arms and legs and noses included.

Mr. Reilly took Harris kite flying one time. They didn't own a kite but stopped at a drug store and bought one and sat out in the grass under the windy sky. The wind blew very hard. Leaves and trash fluttered across the park and clung to the wire fence. As they tried to put the kite pieces together, the bag with the receipt flew from their hands up into the sky and drifted away. Mr. Reilly kept the receipts for everything he bought. He stashed them into boxes he stored in the crawl space in the roof of the house labeled with their dates. He wanted to be able to prove where his money had gone. Instead of getting upset as the bag drifted away, Mr. Reilly chuckled and whipped his thick fingers through his hair, disturbing the meticulous order he had put his hair in that morning. The wind tossed around the loose strands. As soon as they had the kites stretched over the frames, a red and blue one, the kites heaved up and strained against their strings. They were about to just take off and go up into the air, but Harris clung to his frame and his father clung to his while he threaded the string into Harris' kite and he strung the string properly into his kite. They lay back and let the kites unravel the string as they spiraled up and finally they were a blue and red wedge way up above the park. Harris watched his father roll and unroll the twine as if they were fishing. They just had the kites and they weren't doing anything or eating anything or making anything. They could feel the wind coming over the park and pulling up their kites and way above them, their kites floated in the outermost part of the sky where the clouds raced.

Harris never drank coffee with his father. At sixteen, Harris finally got away to Seattle, away from Tacoma where his father had worked sometimes as a plumber and sometimes as a barrista after he was fired from the delivery job. Harris started drinking for himself, even though he was too young to sit in the cafes. He drank because the men he worked with at the docks drank. They drank thermoses full of scalding coffee and Harris didn't think he could get into too much trouble drinking a single cup of weak coffee. After work, they drove to Alki, the beach that overlooked Elliott Bay and the Seattle skyline, and Harris and his buddies sat on the driftwood and drank.

His friends from work didn't say anything, but just sat there and looked at the seagulls walking along the rocky beach turning over seaweed with their beaks. Aside from looking at things, they drank. They smoked cigarettes. They had an understanding among the three of them that things were going to change for them, that something would happen to take them from the job on the docks loading and unloading freighters, or that something about the job would settle down inside them and they would join the other men who took lunch on the pier, spread a table cloth out over a piling, and ate fried chicken and cherries and drank bottles of soda. At lunch the three of them, all new, walked down to the edge of the pier and ate their lunches, hastily packed in their dark rooms before coming to work. They all lived in rooming houses in the south part of the city, a neighborhood that had been tidal flats a hundred years before and still felt wild and marshy, although it also felt ancient now with dusty long machine works, factories, and railyards. They ate their lunch and smoked cigarettes and looked over the black estuary at the end of the pier.

Sometimes a school of fish swarmed through the water, a large living cloud with the little fish loose and silvery and slipping out of view into the murky water. One of the guys hated something about those fish and he would say, "I'm going to catch me some of those grunions and fry them up." He said this while eating his lunch with a sandwich in his hand and his mouth full of egg salad. He took a gulp from his thermos, always drinking coffee at lunch. "Those aren't grunions. I don't know what those are, but those aren't grunions," another of the guys said. This guy disputed everything. They watched the minnows for a little while and then walked back to their jobs. At the end of the day, the three of them stooped and muttered. All they wanted was to go home and sleep. The guy who disliked the fish said, "I'm going home and I'm looking up grunion. Those were grunions and I hate grunions."

There was nothing in their lives, so they hung onto every little thing, an argument over a five dollar loan, over an odd turn of phrase, anything could result in a fistfight.

One of the old workers adopted Harris one day after he had worked there for a month. "So how is the new fella holding up?"

Harris said, "All right, I suppose. But I'm just wondering when I'm going to get used to this work?"

The old hand laughed. "You don't get used to the work. The work just wears into you and you can stand it because you have to stand it. You get addicted to that paycheck, that steady cash and the things you can do to alleviate the weight of this work. That's what happens. You find ways to get by."

"That doesn't sound like a job for people."

"It's the best paying job someone like us is liable to find. Used to be you could work timber, and that would be like this. Timber or fishing and now this is the only thing a decent person can stand, because you can live in the same place and don't have to go out and live in a lumber camp, and besides, all of the trees have been cut down and all of the fish have been fished. But, for some reason, all of this shit still arrives on the dock and we have to unload the shit and pack the shit and get the shit ready. We have a lot of control over the flow of shit into and out of this country, so we get paid shit. It's just plain heavy shit, when you get down to it."

Harris began to go to some of the same place, these old longshoremen went right after work. They spent the evenings drinking coffee and singing and finally crawling home to their rooms in Columbia City or the International District.

His first month became his first year and gradually, Harris needed the draw of a drink to withstand the painful shuffle out of his bed and into the kitchen. He no longer fell asleep buzzing and woke with a painful spastic start, but woke because he needed to get the scalding water dripping through fresh grounds onto the hot plate. He drank mugs of coffee for breakfast and an egg hardboiled green and left in the refrigerator to the point of rotting.

He didn't spend his money. He began to work longer hours to stave off the eventual weary ritual of settling down in his booth in the café and drinking coffee. When the tin box where he stuffed his extra money filled up, Harris figured he needed to put his money in a bank. He opened the account in a marble building downtown and wore his job interview suit, which was now too small in the shoulders and too large in the waist because he spent all of his days lifting the things coming in at the docks. The account manager sat at her desk. She wore a floral dress and a suit jacket and wire-rimmed glasses and smiled at him and put her hands with long polished nails over his hands. "Thank you," she said, "for coming by the bank." She handed him a card and only when he stood out on the sidewalk did he turn the card around and notice that she had written another telephone number on the back. He went to a payphone and called the number. "Hello, you have reached Marjorie Maynard. Please leave a message at the beep." He left a message saying he would be at the Frontier Room at 5:30. Then he went home and changed and went back to the docks.

Marjorie Maynard sat at the table in the Frontier Room window when he came in. She drank with him for a little while and then said, "Let's get something to eat, on me." So he went with her and had something to eat at a nice restaurant and then they walked in the park and sat under a statute and necked. Her lipstick tasted like chalk. Her skin smelled like lemons. Her breasts were coated with a faint white powder that stuck to his tongue. He went home with his face aching and his head happy and drank a cup before going to bed even though he didn't want to.

He desired Marjorie Maynard. He coveted Marjorie Maynard. He had a hankering for this woman. He had a deep thirst in his protoplasm. His heart pumped red blood cells and replenished the oxygen, but could not supply Marjorie Maynard. By this time, he had a deep dedication to his schedule, to his drinking, to his accumulation of money and he was afraid she would make him stop drinking and she would make him spend some of his money on her. He thought her over. He thought maybe he wanted to stop drinking anyway. He never drank because he was thirsty. He called her and told her he would be out of town for a week, but he wanted to see her when he got back. He didn't go to work. Instead, he locked himself in his room. He locked himself in and waited. He first stocked up on liver and corn. He stocked up on apple juice and bananas. He had blankets and he didn't have beans or grounds or even instant crystals and he didn't have a French press, Mr. Coffee, or percolator, or even a filter. He saw it as a matter of will and didn't understand that it wasn't a matter of will, but of addiction and he was addicted and addiction meant a whole lot of things besides the caffeine. He waited and when he wanted a cup really, really bad, he would play back Marjorie's message on the answering machine. He memorized the syllables of her voice until, instead of calling her machine, he could make the sound of her voice in his throat. He transferred his addiction from coffee to the sound she made saying her name. Between the first syllable and the second, between mar and jor, she made a back of the throat growl. Over the week, Harris reduced her name to that noise she made shifting from an R to a J, a sound not really associated with any letter of the alphabet.

Finally, after a week of reading books and drawing

cartoons, Harris felt ready to go out into the world. He went to a café and ordered a glass of warm milk. "A latté is a latté with or without a shot of espresso, my friend. Can I interest you in a decaf latté? It costs as much whether or not it has a shot in it. You should have the shot."

"No thank you," Harris said. "I'm a sober man now. I'm a free man now." He drank his milk and looked at the long bar that seemed somehow dingy in the daylight through clear eyes.

He walked out onto the sidewalk and walked through the city which seemed overall a little shabbier and dirtier and more crummy than he remembered it. Even the smell coming from Puget Sound, normally a salty workman-like smell didn't smell that way to him now, it smelled like rotting fish and old shoes.

He passed the bank where Marjorie worked and peeked inside and saw her working at her desk and it occurred to him that as a sober man he could do better than her. He could do a lot better than her. He already had the thing he liked about her, he'd already discovered it, that sound between R-J. Marjorie, herself, was heavy and a little plain. She wore a mask of meticulously applied make-up. When she walked across the bank, her left ankle wobbled away from her body like it hadn't been fastened correctly to her left knee. He left the bank and walked across the city's central plaza filled with the pan pipes and squeaky voices of a Peruvian band. He sat on a bench under the simulated ancient ruins.

Women walked across the square, and he noticed that almost every other one was a better specimen than Marjorie. But finally, because he didn't know how to meet one of these better specimens, even though the city was crawling with them, he went back to his room and called Marjorie. The voice on her answering machine, which had pulled him through his cold turkey, almost caused him to retch now. He left a message for her and then he lay down on the bed and stared at the ceiling. He didn't know what to do with himself. He suddenly had all of this time before him where he could do anything, except drinking; and drinking had become the only thing he could do with his free time. What would he do, because he had never really wanted to do anything.

Marjorie called and they arranged to meet at the Red Diner. When he arrived, she was there already. She had ordered him a café americano and he said, "Thank you, but I quit drinking."

"Why?" she asked him.

"Because of you," he said.

In the week her voice had been such a focus, the dialogue of getting himself to quit, that he hadn't realized that she didn't really know him. He knew a lot about her voice, having listened to it over and over again. He knew when she pronounced a long A, it pulled back and almost became a short E.

"Can you have decaf?" she said.

"I don't know. I don't think it's recommended, if you have a problem," he said.

"I don't date bean fiends," she said. She placed a twenty on the table and leaned over and kissed him, collected her things, and left.

He watched her leave and then she was gone and he looked around at the people sitting at the other tables. They were either on cell phones talking to people across the town or country, people that were somewhere else, or they were with other people and they were talking to them. Harris was completely alone.

Harris Reilly started with the chocolate-covered bean on her mocha and then drank the mocha and then the americano she had ordered him. He went back to the Frontier Room and his job the next day. For a moment the city had almost seemed as if it would shed its old self and become a new place for him. He wanted to have new, good habits in a new city, but he had bad habits in his old city. He worked hard at the docks and then went out drinking to wake under gray drizzle near a freeway underpass with a swollen bruised face from a poorly remembered fist fight. Someone had not only pulled the pockets out of his pants, but cut them out so that his pockets were just holes in his jeans. His lips were clotted closed with dried blood. His internal organs ached. He didn't know what he wanted to do, just what he didn't want to do. He didn't want to drink coffee. He tried to remember the sound that Marjorie's answering machine made, but he couldn't even remember her telephone number. When she said her name, she made a sound somewhere between R and J. Without a letter, he had no way to find it.

Trap

There were homeless people living in the upper part of the parking garage, where they could easily go in and out, until the super, god bless him, hired the Resident Agent of The Bureau of Extermination. The homeless had quite a hoe-down going on in middle of the night, banjos, bongos, accordions, and cat calls. The Agency posted a notice on the door in large, all capital type, announcing, *Waiver of Liability*. The Agency installed a special trap in the middle of the parking garage. The sign urged tenants to stay clear of the garage, and not even to stray downwind from the garage. Naturally, the man complied up until a couple of days ago, when he noticed that the homeless person problem hadn't improved, but had become worse. At night, lines of ragged strangers shuffled into the garage. More troubling, still, was the coming and going of the brown Agency van. During the night, he looked out and saw the van rattle out of the garage and turn onto the street. The Interurban Extermination Agency had painted their cheerful yellow logo on the van roof, a bright yellow cockroach with a red X over its head. The man had a mind to complain to the super about that van, because it needed a new muffler.

No longer did he hear the music of the homeless people as he went to work in the morning. No longer did he hear that faintly haunting guitar chords and the growling moan of their weird songs. During the day, everything seemed pretty quiet. That was when he noticed that the papers had begun to accumulate on several of the doorways down the hall and that the super did not respond to his note.

He went down to the front desk and didn't notice the super. He went outside and smelled something wonderful cooking, some wonderful smell the man hadn't noticed before. Someone was cooking some incredibly exotic aromatic dish, vanilla. Maybe it was a cake or muffins or cookies or a savory tea? He tried to follow the smell, but it seemed to be coming from the garage where he knew it couldn't be coming from. He circled the building and it must have been coming from the basement and out through the parking garage. He went into the parking garage and the smell, he didn't know how, grew even stronger; his mouth began to water. A delicious hunger and appetite grew in him and he wanted to bury himself in the almond vanilla scent. A black velvet curtain hung over some sort of structure in the middle of the parking garage. It was empty now except for a discarded tennis shoe and a couple of leaves of the daily paper. A faint, flickering light, like a flame perhaps, came from the structure. The man decided the construction must be a tent and he was certain then that the smell came from under its flaps. Maybe someone was making white chocolate? As he approached, the smell grew, until the man thought if he could bury his head into a bucket of chocolate covered almonds and eat until his stomach exploded, he would. He threw back the fabric and found the super with his head buried in a five-by-six-foot brick of whitish, aromatic material. A man wearing a single tennis shoe had buried his head in the block. Before the man thought anything, he buried his head in the stuff, as silly as this seems, because he was afraid they would eat it all. It tasted beyond his wildest expectations and he ate mouthfuls, until substance stuffed his esophagus. He wouldn't remove himself even if he could, because if he died through self-gratification, so be it. If this was extermination, he thought, exterminate me.

Relapse

Harris Reilly came to a strange building he had never seen before to get control over his own life, because in a sense the familiar, the tired and expected routines of his former life, the habits of his former life might change in a new neighborhood. He didn't know anyone in this part of the city. He didn't really look around for anyone or anything. He just made do because he had to escape from his addiction. When he first arrived at the strange building, he checked in with the manager at the front desk. The manager smiled at him and handed him the keys.

He walked up the stairs instead of taking the elevator, noting the fresh paint, the swept walkway, the orderly succession of hallway lights free of dust and cobwebs. Harris Reilly lay down on the refinished hardwood floor. He stared at the ceiling and fell asleep. When he woke, it was dark outside. Music came from the courtyard. Tables for the restaurant had been set out with wicker chairs. In the bathroom, a long insect with enormous whiskers had crawled out of the drain. Even though he washed it back down the drain, the tap issued an orange and red fluid full of black insects, lint, and assorted unidentified floating objects. He waited for the tap to run clear. He filled the tub and sat in the hot water until his skin warmed.

The atmosphere in this part of the city was hard for him to understand. The southern part, next to the ocean smelled like salt and kelp and the forests that grew up into the mountains. Here, the air didn't really move but sat in cool air pockets collecting water and insects. Walking through the streets, he swallowed these things until they filled his stomach and he had to retch on the bloated grass. Water trickled from his pores. A steady drizzle drifted down from the low laying clouds. The clouds sat just over the tops of the buildings, slowly leaking a precipitation that was neither mist nor rain, but a sort of midway moisture. The building walls collected runoff and mold.

When he went walking in the damp city, he tried to keep on the dry side of the street, even thought it was futile because the damp permeated everything. From the front of his building, he passed along the side of a green park with blue grass. No one stood on the grass and there weren't any signs saying keep off grass, it was just assumed that everyone stayed safe inside, crouched next to the electrical heaters drinking hot drinks. That was why he had left his own comfortable neighborhood.

Here, the drinking habits of the locals seemed slightly different. Easy enough to figure out if the pressure of getting some drink became something he wanted to do, but he didn't want to decipher the architecture and figure out where the folks did their drinking. On his walk, he walked over crusty dried filters packed with spent grounds, shattered Frappuccino bottles, and thick heavy bottle bottoms that looked like spectacles for the severely handicapped, cracked and broken in the gutter. Brown paper bags molded to the shapes of the bottles that had been emptied and broken on the side walk. The bags filled the nooks behind the apartment building stoops. He passed men, their beards matted and gray, sprawled on the sidewalk or lying in the crosswalks where they had fallen the night before. Harris wanted to stop and help them to their feet and tell them to leave this city and to go away. How could they go? It had cost him so much to move himself here and install himself in his apartment, that he imagined these drunks were locked in the inertia of their addiction.

They drank everything they could get their hands on, turning old chest-of-drawers, suits, work shoes with the leather polished and buffed into cash. The cash easily transformed into a furtively procured shot of espresso, leaving behind a quickly fading buzz and crème mustache. There was just time to kill and they killed it one swallow at a time and when they woke in the morning with their spines stiff from sleeping on the crooked pavement, they hurried under shelter where they waited in a long line to get some soup and crackers or whatever it was that people ate in this neighborhood. Harris wanted to sit in the long warm café with the steamy hiss of an espresso machine. He wanted the sparkling ornaments behind the bar. He wanted the people like himself to talk to and now he didn't have anyone to talk to. He kept stopping at crosswalks when the light was against him, but the foot traffic just kept flowing across the street because there weren't any cars coming. He realized that this neighborhood had the same problems, even worse, because in these cafés they offered sanctuary from the damp and desolate, fractured sidewalks.

Finally, he stopped, freezing and exhausted, and went through a narrow door and found himself in a place with a gigantic wooden bar. The barrista told him that this gigantic wooden structure had come around The Cape of Good Hope. That was how old it was. It was in the city long enough that a sailing ship had carried it around the Cape. And it was brought all the way up the coast to Seattle to provide a civilization to the frontier. This civilization in the form of a hardwood bar still sat here in Seattle and accumulated dust and a patina of spilled drinks. The frontier wasn't even a memory. Civilization moved outward from the core of the city, leaving behind empty buildings and a wilderness of vacant lots. Harris ordered a cup of coffee and drank. The wintry core of damp air left his lungs.

Humanbrain

Business Plan: Humanbrain will expand to over fifty locations in the next year. In a plan endorsed by the Catholic Church and applauded by conservationists, Humanbrain will convert derelict monasteries and convents into functioning recovery and training centers. Low construction costs, unlimited labor, adds up to explosive growth.

Mission Statement: Humanbrain by combining cutting edge computer network solutions with forward oriented health-care strategies, offers insurance companies the lowest cost, top-tier addiction recovery programs. Our program graduates motivated and globally competitive workers in the information industry.

Facilities: Humanbrain offers comfortable live-in campuses modeled after the classic higher education campus, with the facilities to handle late-stage addiction recovery, and skills training bunkers that are the envy of regional vocational schools. Students have access to the latest next-gen workstations using business standard software, provide by an in-kind donation from Microsoft.

Recovery Rates: Students graduate from Humanbrain free of harmful addiction. Because we provide employment, we have a one hundred percent retention rate. Relapses simply do not happen using Humanbrain's patented process. Step 1) Lock down rehabilitation to separate the addict from the addiction. Step 2) Replace harmful addiction to substance to helpful addiction to computer. Step 3) Train addict in dataprocessing. Step 4) Install the addict in home at workstation to repay the cost of recovery.

A Problem with Authority

H arris Reilly was going to go cold turkey once and for all. He was willing to take whatever it took to get clean. He went to the grocery store and bought himself a fifty-pound bag of potatoes, five pounds of butter, salt, pepper. He bought himself frozen chicken breasts and the daily paper so he would have something to read when he got to where he was going to go. When he arrived, he would have to wait it out and kick the coffee habit. He was afraid, though, that once he made it past the physical addiction, he would never get past the non-physical addiction. He had stepped through the other side of it, really. He might lose the nickel-bite at the back of his throat. He might recoil at the thought of a hot drink of bitter, black Joe, even though he was sure he would always love the smell of a coffee shop, especially the smell of espresso in a bookshop where the odor of ink, paper pulp, and dust mixed with the steam forced through roasted coffee ground. That was the smell he could not get out of his nose. Even the smell of a newspaper, acidic paper pulp, held associations for the substance he craved.

He could not go back to being un-addicted. There wasn't even a word for being un-addicted. He could describe the state he wanted only through negating the word addiction.

A virgin was a virgin; an addict was an addict. There was no such thing as an unvirgin.

He wanted to be the way he had been before he'd swallowed his first cup. He'd begun drinking coffee at Denny's, even though he knew his old man had a problem. For a long time, Harris didn't drink coffee because he knew once he started drinking, it wouldn't stop. He knew what it smelled like, but he wouldn't drink it. When he had been in Seattle and the other guys had been drinking coffee from thermoses on the docks, he decided he needed a drink himself. He figured if he didn't keep it in the house, if he didn't drink it at work, he wouldn't have trouble. If he purposefully experimented with it at Denny's, everything would be all right, right? Coffee was too pervasive a substance for him not to come to terms with it. He ordered a cup and some waffles. The waitress brought him the waffles and the coffee. When he drank the coffee, Harris wanted the cup to be unpleasant, so he didn't add milk or sugar. When he'd finished this single cup, the waitress, without even asking him if he wanted more, topped the empty cup off with a fresh dose. He felt obliged to finish up what he'd been served. He meant to put his hand over the lid of the cup and say something like "that'll do," but when he did, the waitress was serving a couple across the aisle or discussing something in a hushed voice with the short-order cook. Harris felt the warm lip of the mug. He felt the steam rise from the cup and condense on the palm of his hand. He went back to reading his book. The waitress, without so much as a hello, filled his cup.

Harris finally left, jittery and euphoric. He had drunk a lot of coffee. His head felt sort of loose and shaky, as if the skin had separated slightly from his scalp. He went home and sprawled in bed. He couldn't fall asleep. He boiled some milk on the stove and poured the milk from the soup pan in a long, frothy arc into a mug. He drank the warm milk, belched, and watched the shadows move on the ceiling until morning and he thought that was it, he was never going to be addicted to coffee. He believed he'd somehow lucked out with his genetic disposition for addiction and he was not addicted to coffee. He hated coffee, in fact. His genetic heritage, being Irish, made him far more liable to addiction than just about any other nationality, and that predisposition for addiction had somehow passed him. He went to work and felt like crap. When the boys poured themselves their coffee at work, he didn't have any, but by the end of the day he was so tired that when he went back to Denny's he asked for a cup of coffee and when the waitress poured it, he could almost feel the little caffeine receptors open up in the lining of his stomach. Instead of stopping at the first cup, or being surprised when the waitress came around to fill up the cup again, he was amazed this time by how she took her time to scoop up the coffee pot and the extraordinary length of time it took for coffee to pour out of the pot and into the mug.

Harris Reilly took his groceries and drove into a remote corner of the Cascade Mountains, on a highway that used to see a lot of traffic before the federal government punched Interstate-90 through the Snoqualmie Pass in the 1970s. His father used to drive the family out to a deserted camping ground. While his father poured gasoline into the fire pit to get the damp logs burning, Harris remembered feeding the camp-robbers. They skittered down from the mossy trees and would jump almost within arms reach for him to feed. He tore up pieces of stale bread and fed them. He tore up the hotdog buns until his father grumbled and grabbed them out of his hands. "Those are for people, not goddamn birds."

The area Harris drove to used to see a lot of tourists before the timber companies cut all of the trees down. The highway followed the path of a broad riverbed filled with an intermittent trickle of water. On the other side of the river, Harris could see an even older road cut into the valley wall. Sometimes the track disappeared where it crossed a mud bank or a very active geological area and then reappeared where a stand of old trees protected the hillside from sliding. There the old road looked like it must have looked years ago when cars still drove along it. He came to a motel in a dank hollow. If he hadn't been looking for the motel, he'd have missed it. Harris remembered the place very well. His father had moved the family there during a rainstorm during one of their hiking trips and Harris remembered sitting at the indoor picnic tables in the large hallway filled with other families driven out of the mountains by the rain. Everyone ate sandwiches. Someone played a banjo and that was particularly remarkable, because they didn't play "Sweet Chariot" or "Sweet Georgia Brown" but could actually play and sing and they played and sang. There was something about that moment, uninformed as it was by his father's growing coffee habit and their sudden transition from the damp, empty campsite that smelled like the gasoline Harris' father poured into the fire pit. Even so, it had been so damp, not even the gas burned for long.

Harris' motel room was rarely used and smelled only of woodsmoke and the faint odor of mold. An old fridge ticked and groaned in the open kitchen. A thick, yarn-like shag carpet bear-hugged every inch of the floor. Chenille bedspreads covered the twin beds. They had the bulk of two child-sized coffins. The motel proprietor followed Harris around the room. She wore faded lavender pants, a threadbare green cardigan. Her hair rose in a stacked, gray beehive. With her pale skin and hair, she looked slightly carbonized, as if she had fallen into the stove and been left there for the winter. In stark contrast, she wore a quilted, don't-shoot-me, orange hunting coat over everything else. Harris nodded at her and she stepped out onto the porch to smoke. She looked at the light falling through the branches up on the trees growing up on the western wall of the valley. The light shown down in a wide patch on the eastern wall of the valley, completely missing the valley floor and the wide entrance to the camp ground where Harris' father used to take him as a child. "You ain't a hunter, are you," she said, not as a question but as a point of fact.

"No," he said.

"What are you doing up this way?"

"I need a quiet place to think things out."

"This is as quiet as it comes. It's so quiet that it's loud. Things you don't hear in normal places get on your nerves. Leaves rustle in the city. Sort of a pleasant sound, as I recall. Out here, the leaves play maracas. They sound like a big brass band. You can't shut the leaves up. Quiet, I think, is a relative thing."

"Yes," Harris said. "That is what I'm looking for. Quiet."

"It isn't hunting season now, in case you are a hunter and I got you figured wrong. It's even quiet up here when it's hunting season. Ain't nothing up here to kill, you see."

"Yes," he said. "I'm not hunting. Just looking for a quiet place to mull over some things."

"Would you like to come inside and have a cup of coffee? I just made a pot. I can't drink a whole pot. It'll just have to go to waste. Although, to be honest, sometimes I leave it out overnight. In the morning, I heat it up on the hot plate. That can't be good for a person." She flicked her smoking cigarette out into the parking lot. "I made this coffee just a while ago, in case you think I'm trying to foist some week-old bilge off on you."

"I don't know. Coffee is not supposed to be that good for you, regardless."

"I was reading," she said, "that if you drink it within fifteen minutes of when you brewed it, it has anti-cancer agents. A whole lot of them. But who drinks their coffee within fifteen minutes? I wonder how long it really lasts, really. If it is good for you one minute, it can't go to being bad for you the next." She lit another cigarette. "I'll be manning the fort if you'd like some company or a cup of coffee."

Harris pushed the two small beds together and lay across them. He had trouble sleeping because he could hear, in the absence of street noise, the rattle of leaves on the trees, the echoing gurgle of the river, the shotgun crack of the motel's settling timbers. He turned and dozed and turned and dozed and then woke after his sleeping body wedged between the two beds and he bounced onto the thick shag carpet. He could feel the receptors in his body muttering coffee bean coffee bean coffee bean. Harris made himself a cup of decaf instant coffee. He sipped it and sat on the motel porch, overlooking a gully. A wild creek burbled through the rocks at the bottom of the cleft. The moon lit the fringes of the clouds. Harris wandered over to the motel office and found the door open. Inside, he saw a typewriter, a rotary phone, and the coffee maker. The practically full coffee pot still had a little heat in it. Harris drank the whole pot. He held the pot up to his mouth and then drank it down, spilling coffee over his T-shirt and underwear. When he was done, he staggered back to his room, pushed the two beds back together, and then he sat on the couch. He was too tired not to lie down and too wired not to sleep.

At dawn, he showered, and then drove himself to the first hospital. He saw the square blue H sign on the highway, and then drove into the parking lot. He double checked the lock on his car door. Trembling, he went into the emergency room. He said he needed to turn himself over. He said he was afraid for his life. He said he needed help. The nurse led him into an examination room. Finally, a doctor looked at him. The doctor asked if Harris would wait for a van that would be there in a half an hour. "There is a little formality," the doctor said, "we have to take care of."

"Yes?"

"Are you powerless over this substance?"

"I am."

"Do you commit yourselves to our care?"

"I do."

"Do you relinquish your rights to an attorney?"

"I do."

"Do you relinquish your right to a phone call?"

"Help me."

"Do you?"

"I do."

Harris waited in the waiting room. They had taken his clothes and given him a blue, paper jumpsuit and a wristband. A Mexican man and his two children sat in the waiting room with Harris. The man smiled and Harris nodded back. Then the man's wife came through the swinging doors leading into the examination rooms. She had long dark hair and a double chin and the man took her by the funnybone and led her out and the two children followed him. "Let's get out of this nuthouse," the man said.

At long last, a man came in with a baseball cap and a yellow jacket on. The yellow jacket said Humanbrain. He talked to the nurse and laughed. He chewed gum. He had a very wrinkled face, short hair on the sides of his skull, and a long mane dripping all of the way down to his back collar. He had a black plastic watch and when he came up to Harris, he presented Harris with a rectangle of plastic with a blinking light and a plastic stick. "Can you sign this, please?"

Harris signed the device. His signature filled a smooth luminous panel. The man asked Harris if he had any bags or anything.

"I have my car."

"Number on the license plate?"

Harris followed the man out to a van and sat down. Several other people were already in the van. They looked out of the windows at the darkening sky at the sides of the mountains. In a few places, the mountains came way down and had clear-cuts with a few stray trees. Their limbs were stark against the falling daylight. The inside of the van smelled like carpet and plastic and talcum powder. Harris felt wonderful just sitting down. The man helped Harris put on his seat belt and then he slid the door closed and was on his way. No one else in the van said anything they were all lost in their own private thoughts, looking at the top of the mountain ridges. The van eased out onto the road and then onto the highway and kept going for a long time. A radio kept the driver informed of the other vans pick-ups being conducted at Overlake and Tukwila and Hoquaim. After a long time, the van pulled off the freeway and drove past a strip-mall, then turned into a private drive, under a stand of dark firs. Yards lights were planted in the ground and glowed up through the ferns and the trunks of very large old, trees. The van pulled into a gothic monastery quad.

An old man who said he was The Quartermaster led Harris down a hallway. "You will sign out for the blankets," the man said. "You will sign out for the radio. You will sign out for every article of clothing and you will give me what you have. You will not say a word."

"I don't want a radio."

"You don't have to have a radio," he said. "You don't need to listen to anyone's voice at all. You can just sit in your cell and look out at the clouds and think about what you have done to find yourself here, partner."

The Quartermaster led Harris into a narrow hallway that stretched all of the way to the ceiling stuffed with blankets. Each blanket was folded neatly into a tight square and went all of the way up toward the ceiling. A different pattern or fabric made each of the blankets. A few quilts rested interspersed in the wall of multicolored blankets. When Harris reached out to take a red blanket, The Quartermaster said, "No, not that one. You don't have any right to take that one."

"Don't I have to sign for it? So can't I take any one I like?"

"You'll sign for the blanket we assign to you. You don't have any right taking any one you want. That is the first lesson you will need to learn. You won't get by for one second here being greedy. This is a store." The Quartermaster reached down and pulled out a dusty, thin, wool army blanket. Harris had his hand on a thick quilted blanket folded neatly a little higher than he could reach unless he stood on his tip toes. He had his hand out and had his fingers over the blanket and he was pulling it out of its spot in the wall of blankets when The Quartermaster stopped him and pulled out this other blanket and told him he would have to have this olive green thing. He sure didn't want the olive drab thing when he could have a blanket like that quilt.

He took the blanket The Quartermaster assigned to him and signed out for his pajamas without trying them on. Harris found himself in a small room. He sat down. The Quartermaster told him the Orientation Director would show him around in the morning when it got light. While Harris slept that night, he could hear the howl of the wind coming down over the lake and through the branches of the tall fir trees. Against the window panes, the wind sounded hollow and large and it hissed. Gusts of air forced cold drops of water through the window molding and blew around the room. He could feel the specks of water. In the distance, he could hear someone singing and then howling and then singing and finally late at night, when a gust of wind woke him, Harris realized they had stopped. It was just getting light outside and he heard an alarm in the distance, metal on metal and then it faded. He thought he heard the barking of dogs. Then he lay in the bed in the cool gray morning light, not sure what to do with himself.

He sat back in bed and listened to the doors down the hallway open and slam shut. "Wake up." Someone knocked on his door. "Time for your shower."

Harris grabbed his shower bag. Everything was in vacuum-sealed containers with the words Humanbrain printed on the plastic case. He walked down the windowless hallways and into the mutely lit, tiled bathroom. He opened the case and threw it into the bathroom trash. The mirror wasn't glass, but a piece of remarkably highly polished metal bolted to the wall. The sink faucets turned on when he put his hands under them. He stood in the shower and couldn't adjust the heat. The water came out and it was just a little too cold, so he didn't stay in the shower for as long he would have liked to have stayed under hot water. Instead, he shivered and scoured the soap on himself and rinsed off and, when he came out, Harris smelled like ginger and mustard from the soap that Humabrain.com had provided for him. He brushed his teeth. While he had his mouth open and listening to the scrub scrub of the new toothbrush bristles on his molars, a woman in a yellow track suit came into the bathroom and told everyone in there to stop there lollygaggingaround and to come out to the breakfast table. Harris followed, leaving his Humanbrain things in the bathroom and followed the group down a flight of stairs and into a cafeteria lit nicely with outdoor light coming down through skylights. They ate oatmeal for breakfast and orange juice. His gums hurt; he wanted a cup of coffee.

Harris looked around at the other people. Everyone was dressed in grayish sweat clothes and when they stood up, they began to put on their hoods in preparation for outdoors.

"Partner Harris Reilly," the woman in the yellow track suit yelled.

"That's me," he said.

She smiled at him. "You can address me as your partner. We are all in this together. Say 'Here I am, partner,' like a good partner."

"Here I am, partner."

"You left your things in the bathroom. Please secure them in your room."

When Harris went to the bathroom, he saw that his things had been neatly folded back into the pouch. The pouch looked identical to the pouches everyone else had. How did they know it was his?

Everyone walked around the track for a long time. A fine mist fell out of the sky and soaked the grass. The grass had long heavy drops of rain water. The track held a thick, liquid mud that coated their shoes. When they were done, they were lead back inside and could go back to their rooms. While he was gone, someone had placed three books on his bed in a vacuum-pack sealed package including a pen. The first booklet explained what he had to do. First, he had to pass a written placement test and then he had to follow the instructions to find out what he could do for Humanbrain once they had done what they could do for him. Then he needed to understand and learn to live by the rules.

Rule 1: You are an addict. An addict is addicted to addiction and even when the addict loses the craving for a particular substance they cannot lose the craving for addiction. The benefit of substituting an activity for the substance is that you can turn your addiction into a helpful compulsion. There may be no way to escape addiction. But you can put addiction to work for yourself.

Rule 2: Don't use cuss words. Cussing is a gateway activity. One action lends itself to another action. Swearing is the foundation for all counterproductive activity. Before you say anything you should formulate what it is you're saying. If you're using the word *fuck*, do you really mean the word *fuck*? Do you really mean *fornication*? Because that is what *fuck* means, or do you mean something else? You can't possibly mean *fornication* as many times as you say, *fuck*. You probably mean something else. A recovered addict thinks through his thoughts before s/he says what s/he needs to say. An addict has a lot more on his or her mind than a normal person. Inhibition is important to an addict. Consider yourself. Censor yourself. Don't speak your mind until you know your mind.

Rule 3: Eat the proscribed diet. Just as you can't take any filth out of your mouth, you can't put any filth into your mouth. Everything you ingest has wide reaching social, political, and pharmacological ramifications. You cannot put what you want into your mouth until you consider what you are putting into your mouth. Don't believe what you read. Consult the approved authorities before you eat anything.

"You have, Partner Reilly," his therapist told him at the conclusion of his briefing, "I'm sorry to say, a problem with authority."

"I have a lot of things wrong with me. I'm an addict. Sure. But I don't have a problem with authority."

"We've evaluated you. This is our diagnosis. Are you disagreeing with us?"

"I'm disagreeing with you."

"Mmmm," he said. He typed something into his computer. They sat in a mutely lit office. A soft natural sound came from the matte black speakers. An apple cinnamon odor filled the room. The desk was a heavy black arrangement and the chairs were thick and plush, but very firm. Harris sat on one of the firm chairs and felt comfortable, except for the burning withdrawal headache. His therapist sat at the desk and he had a digital file open and Harris could see his photograph on it, from the night he had arrived from the hospital.

The woman in the yellow track suit brought Harris a cup of decaf coffee and three small pills. She said, "This is the caffeine you are dependent on. This is what it looks like. This is poison and you are dependent on poison. Eat it up."

The coffee grew worse and worse as the week went on. Harris set in the cell and it would grow cold and the finally he would sip it because he was bored and this is what he always did to take the edge of things. The pills gradually went from black to gray, until finally, they were white and he knew they weren't really doing anything for him, but he ate them anyway. Each day, he had to go to exercise. He had to go to training session where they learned how to open windows, and to double-click the mice, how to drag and drop icons, and then finally how to type and enter information into the database. That first day, when he was at the computer, they bought him a cup of perfect coffee. And every day after that, his coffee grew worse. He still anticipated the computer and the coffee, and as the coffee grew worse he grew fond, very fond indeed, of his computer.

He maintained the secret vice of calling Marjorie's answering machine to hear her say her own name, to hear that odd sound that doesn't have a letter of the alphabet, between R and J. And then one day she was home during the day. She said, "Hello, this is Marjorie," and when she said it this time, her own name, she completely missed the sound that Harris craved.

"Hi, this is Harris." He told her about his life at Humanbrain.

"I don't date addicts," she said.

"You dated me when I was drinking coffee."

"You weren't an addict, then. You were using but you didn't think of yourself as addicted to coffee until you tried to quit. Addicts are no fun."

Wild Animal Ears

Wild animal ears need to hear free air. This is a well known fact. An ear drum embedded in a caged animal can't hear the vital things a wild animal can hear. Wild animals hear the rustle of fir needles, the hush of snow accumulating on snow as each flake individually collides into a field of serrated ice crystals, or the rattle of wind down a stony crevasse. A caged animal can just listen to its own heart beat or its own incessant panting or its own howling, which was the case for the trapped animal Harris Reilly and his father found at the foot of the mountain. Harris couldn't really tell what kind of wild animal it was, except it was a four-legged mammal with a snout and bluish hair. Perhaps it was a coyote or a even a wolf.

Harris' father chortled when Harris suggested the trapped wild animal might be a wolf. "That ain't no wolf. Wolf hasn't been in Washington State since World War I, and even then it was only something you heard about from someone else and didn't see yourself." Used to be a trapper earned his living by catching and killing wolves. The State had a bounty on them and the hunters sold the ears to the Government Agents. Each ear represented the whole animal. "It was a matter of practicality," Harris' father said, "because then a hunter didn't have to carry the whole damn animal to the Government Agents."

"What he'd do with all those ears?"

"Probably burned them. What would you do with a bag of wild animal ears?"

Harris thought he'd make a quilt out of them, or something. It seemed a waste to have all of those animals killed and not make any civilized use of them.

Harris and his father stood some way from the wild animal, that was probably a coyote. It had one leg caught in a trap, a pair of steel jaws with thick teeth. The clamp caught the animal right up on its thigh. The animal howled and slobbered and it tried to chewed through its own leg like it no longer wanted to keep this leg that had become a domesticated leg. The other three wild legs wanted to get away.

"What should we do?" Harris asked his father. "Can't we let it go?"

The animal howled and rolled its eyes. Its neck throbbed with the effort of crying out from the pain of the trap clamped onto its leg and from the worry about it must have felt about not being able to move.

Harris' father took a step toward the animal and then stood as best as he could in front of Harris. "The animal belongs to the hunter. The hunter has a right to kill wild animals. We don't have a right to free wild animals once they are caught."

"But it's a wild animal. It's supposed to be free, not in a trap."

The wild animal thrashed and hollered.

Harris walked around his father and toward the beast. It saw him approach and even though Harris wanted to help it, the animal lunged toward him. The skin around its eyes was swollen. Its dark blue fur was matted with froth and slobber. Little specks of blood coated its foamy mane. Blood streamed from the deep gash where the trap had closed on the animal. Blood poured from the scars where the beast had tried to gnaw through its own leg. "It's all right, little guy," Harris said.

The beast panted and then jumped at Harris. The trap, chained to an ingot driven deep into the rocky soil, snapped taut and pulled the animal back. Harris backed away. "What are we going to do?"

"We came here to go up this mountain," his father said. "We're going to go up this mountain. Maybe while we are going along something will occur to us and we will know how to get out of this."

Harris thought his father might be correct. So on the way up the mountain he thought about what he could do. He thought maybe he could shoot a sleeping arrow into the animal's hind haunches using some herbs they could find in the mountains. Harris could remove the trap, and the animal would be fine. Harris' father didn't know anything about mountain flora. Harris thought maybe they could use a stick to knock the animal unconscious and then remove the trap. He began to look for a stick and finally near the top of the mountain he found a heavy, smooth, limb. He dragged that down the mountain behind his father. When they finally arrived at the car, and to the place where the animal had been, they found that even though the hunter hadn't been there, the wild animal had been able to chew through its leg. The discarded leg lay tethered to the trap, civilized, while the animal and its remaining three wild legs were still free.

Seattle Directory Assistance

The first voice Harris heard on his return to Seattle came over the directory assistance line, a smooth woman's voice assuring him that she could get him away from his apartment building, itself a difficult place to find in the confusing and shifting lattice of arterials. Her voice had a smooth nonchalance, a seductive hang at the end of "take a right hand turn on to..." while she paused to name the exact street. Harris wrote the directions to the Humane Society down on the back of a heavy manila card with the lease printed on one side. He wanted to ask her some new questions, more personal questions, something that would give away what she looked like or how old she was, because at this point in their conversation she had remained briskly professional, even a little cold. He cleared his throat. She did nothing. He asked to clarify the directions and she just kept talking. He coughed, a heavy, wet hack and wiped the phone off. She didn't even say excuse *you*. She asked him, "Did you miss any of this transmission?"

"Transmission?" Harris asked, as in what kind of word is transmission? He found this odd, cold word maddening, because he had began to build an idea of what the operator looked like, a woman wearing a dark blue pleated skirt and a white blouse with pearly buttons, and straight blonde hair pulled back in an inlaid pearl barrette, and wire-rim glasses. He realized he had made her out to be the youngish librarian where he used to go after school in Seattle to avoid going back home. Instead of reading, he observed the librarian paging through a magazine and sometimes vaguely smiling at patrons as they dropped their books with a dusty thump onto the wooden checkout counter. His librarian whispered and he didn't know her normal speaking voice, just the polite whisper telling him the dates his books were due. "Transmission?" Harris asked again and in the sure, patient quality, the similarity in the soft pallet flicks and the glottal stops, Harris realized he had become entranced by the Seattle Transportation Authority's automated voice system.

Harris stood in a strange apartment full of boxes of recently purchased goods in a strange city in a strange part of the world, at least for him. He had spent the last year in a treatment program in a converted monastery on a hill overlooking Lake Washington. He spent most of his time training on computers, working through the languages and then the applications, and finally the last three months teaching new partners in the program. Everyone at Humanbrain, the treatment and employment service, referred to everyone else as *partner*. They all wore the same blue oxford, cardigan, and rumpled trousers. Everyone drank a lot of steamed milk, taking their breaks on the cement patio leading into the building, the steam rising from their cups as they huddled in the cool drizzle. No one smoked. The recovery booklet maintained that smoking lead to drinking and drinking was the gateway drug to sloth. Humanbrain did maintain that while there were twelve steps to recovery, in a godless world the only higher authority a lost soul could find was addiction. There was healthy addiction, such as an addiction to exercise. There was unhealthy addiction, such as an addiction to caffeine. Harris did not know the personal stories of the other partners and they didn't know his; and gradually he liked it that way, because they acquiesced all control to the benevolent guidance of Humanbrain, their benefactor, the organization that provided a roof over their heads, a nice little room in one of the converted monk's cells and computer training, and finally a purpose.

The Death of Charlotte Brontë

An account of the awfully sudden death of Charlotte Brontë, a naughty child addicted to falsehood and deceit.

Let me ask: Who is Charlotte Brontë?

She is the parson's daughter.

S he is the quiet, plain daughter of a parson raised in Haworth, a remote village in Yorkshire. In a rigid class system she and her three sisters have neither the income to have guests or to travel, nor the freedom to freely interact with the other citizens of Haworth, so she and her family live in relative isolation. Yet from this relatively unremarkable background, Charlotte becomes the author of *Jane Eyre*, and three other novels under the pseudonym Currer Bell. Her sisters Emily and Anne also write books as Ellis and Acton Bell; however, both die shortly after the publication of their works. Emily dies within the year. It is if they are rare lichen that cannot withstand the direct light of public opinion. With the last Brontë death, hundreds of neighbors visit the parsonage where they were born, reared and died.

She is Currer Bell.

Mr. Bell has a modest income and enjoys spending his Sunday afternoons in reflection while ambulating through his rose garden and down the lane where the rustic country scenes provide many sources of unexpected delight. He frequently pauses to catch his breath because he enjoys his marbled beef and his port and because he slathers his potatoes in butter and will always ask the cook for a second helping of custard. He writes poetry for his own amusement. The dreamy angst of Bell's poetry is an expression of a misspent sense of humor. He lived his early days in India. He refers to this distant period of his life as the immoral adventures of his youth. He writes in the morning and then reads in the afternoon, carefully and unassumingly producing a thick tome every couple of years. Suddenly at the end of the 1840s, Mr. Bell finds all of these books printed under three different pseudonyms. He devised these names so as to confuse his friends and neighbors because they would view his silly novels with shock and disgust and failed to understand the amusement they had provided to Currer over the years.

I must mention his whiskers. His face is a botanical exhibit of whiskered growths, a mustache with exquisitely waxed and sculpted twists at each end, shaggy muttonchops, and a long, neatly trimmed goatee.

It is an unending source of pleasure that he can pass himself of as backward country girl from Yorkshire.

She is The Duke of Wellington.

Nemesis of Bonaparte, she began her military career in India in 1796 and was appointed the supreme commander in the Deccan in 1805. She fought in the Peninsular War and appointed Commander-in-Chief after the death of Sir John Moore. She liberated Spain and Portugal from French control and was created Duke in 1814 after defeating the French at Waterloo.

Charlotte says: Dirty Windows

I often imagine my sisters coming back to me. I watch for their black bonnets coming over the moors. Watching for them, today, I realized that the windows had not been washed for a long time. Droppings clotted with stray strands of feathers and small stones had dried to the window. In fact, all of the windows to the Parsonage were coated in filth, splattered insect bodies, cob webs, the dingy gray pills of gestating moths, and on one pane, I even found a patch of moss and a fully grown fern. The windows had turned fungus farms. "Tabby."

"Yes, ma'am."

I missed her calling me Miss. "The windows are filthy."

"Are they ma'am?"

"When do you think they will be cleaned?"

"I'll get to it as soon as I recover from the TB, ma'am. If you will recall, ma'am, I've just now gained the strength to crawl off my straw pallet and begin some of the housework that has stacked up while I was suffering a spell of the TB."

"The light can barely pass through the dirty window panes."

"Do you remember the view?"

"Yes, Tabby."

"Then, ma'am, you have better memory than that glass. The windows do not have a long memory of staying clean. They dirty themselves up. Don't care whether you see through them or not."

"They are windows," Mr. Nicholls, my dear husband, said. "Does this chair care if I am sitting on it?"

"It would if it knew how much you took it for granted, sir."

Emily had kept the windows so clear, I hadn't even realized they could become dirty. She kept the house cleaner than Martha and Tabby; Martha was careless because this was not her house and she was a young woman who was caring for a blind Parson, my father. His blindness provided for Mary an excuse for idleness. Tabby just could not manage the girl well enough to keep the glass clean.

Mr. Nicholls read the papers in the parlor while he drank his tea. He frowned as I returned from the kitchen with a pail of boiling water and ammonia. "You really should let the girl do that. Your hands are already raw from scrubbing the hallway last night." Emily's knuckle scabs lined the bridges of her fists like barnacles. The joints of her fingers had hardened. She gripped the pen with her fingers and made minute letters as she wrote in the booklets I made for her. I wiped down the surfaces of the glass. I wiped down each stile and then each pane and drew my nail along the molding between the glass and the stile sending a squall through the room. Mr. Nicholls did not say a word. He rattled his paper. The majority of the soot had settled on the outside of the parsonage. I could not adequately clean the windows from indoors.

Rain drops clung to the blades of grass, but the rain had let up. The window was much higher than I anticipated. I needed the pruning stool from the shed. I rattled on the window to get Mr. Nicholls' attention. "Charlotte," he said. I watched him fold the paper and find his spectacles in his breast pocket. He wiped them clean and opened the window. "Yes?"

"I must have the pruning stool."

He looked up at the low clouds. "Perhaps you should come inside?"

With one look from me, he smiled and said, "Yes. I'll get the pruning stool. It is in the shed."

The stool was a gigantic artifact constructed decades ago out of hard wood. It had four iron wheels ostensibly to ease its transport from one end of the yard to the other, but one of the front wheels had rusted to its caster and dragged in the mud. Mr. Nicholls pushed and then dragged the stool across the lawn, grunting and sweating until he had it positioned. The Parsonage had fourteen windows.

By now, my pail of hot water had cooled and a spider had fallen into the bucket and floated like an octopus. I scooped him out in my hand and tossed him aside. I stood on the stool and rinsed down the window. Mr. Nicholls, my dear husband, shrieked. "Ah! A damn spider!" He adjusted his glasses. "Charlotte it is raining."

"I am washing the windows of the house, today."

"Come inside. Your constitution is not great enough to handle inclement weather."

"I am not the one shrieking at spiders," I said.

He stood erect in the middle of the lawn. He held his hand behind his back. I knew he could stand like this for hours. He stood with his back rigid and monitored my progress. Rain drops collected on his spectacles. The clouds rolled overhead, and everything darkened. A wind ruffled the leaves of the shrubs around the house. Small cold drops of heavy rain started to fall. My cherished husband, Mr. Nicholls, did not move. When I climbed down from the stool, he said, "Are you finished?"

"I have the rest of the windows to do. I need more warm water."

Tabby asked me what I was doing. She was in the kitchen cutting up a chicken and peeling vegetables. I'm not sure how she so thoroughly dissolved these seemingly wholesome ingredients into the thin greasy broth she pawned off to my father as soup. "What do you need a big pot of boiling water for, dear?"

"I am washing the outside of the house."

"I can get someone to do that. It is raining and Brontës can't take the cold. Come inside."

"I am washing the outside of the Parsonage."

"You can't see the outside of the Parsonage when you are inside."

"I want to see outside, Tabby."

"Charlotte, there is nothing for you to see out there anyway."

Mr. Nicholls stood silently in the place where I had

left him. He did not offer to help me, except to shove the stool to the next window. "This is eccentric," he said.

"I am an author," I said.

"That is not an excuse."

"You say that to most people around these parts, and they would just nod their head and say yes, so she is, so she is, and let me go on my way and work on this thing. Wanting a clean house is more eccentric in their minds, I'd say."

I say: Glass Town Dope Epidemic

Okay here's the situation. His parent's were not on a week's vacation, and Branwell was still in his room smoking opium. Maybe he shouldn't? Naw—of course, he should.

Branwell at thirty years old sponged off his father while he got stumble down drunk. His father was a Parson; I might add. Maybe Branwell was thinking if Coleridge fried himself on half a bowl, Branwell would toast on an urn of assorted opiates and churn out an Illiad or two. It is all about dosage. Up until the time the Brontës were in their early twenties, Branwell had produced more work than his sisters would produce in the rest of their lives, combined. It was no worse than their writing of the same period, it was just when they began to get serious about writing, Branwell began to get serious about drinking.

Charlotte says: Yellow

We were used to smoke coming from Branwell's chamber, but before he set himself on fire, an incident occurred that should have warned us that Branwell had fallen into the final stage of dissipation. Yellow vapors escaped from his room. At first, this cloud had a somewhat pleasant odor but it gradually gained strength until the overpowering stench was obviously something toxic. How could he stand the reek within his room where it must be double-fold in intensity? I could barely stand the tearful stink at the foot of the stairs.

We gathered before his door holding napkins to our faces. "Branwell? What in God's name are you doing?" His door opened, and the stench became so thick it was a floating distortion of the atmosphere like the air above a boiling teapot; the lines of the hallway moldings distorted and twisted and snapped free. Everything seemed slower and blurred as water, tears, and sweat began to drip from our hair. "Branwell how do you live with that smell?" The stink at his door was the innards of the infected anthrax riddle sheep we saw slaughtered near Haworth, its thick black bile leaking like odoriferous mud from an incision in the poor creature's stomach. The yellow gas issued from Branwell's room leaving powder trails around the door frame. He finally opened his door completely, sending out a solid wall of brown smoke. We rushed down the hallway, gagging on our napkins while Branwell rubbed one hand over his swollen belly, distended and throbbing around his puckered belly button. He squinted at us through his bloated eyes. He leaned forward and held up a long glass cylinder discharging even more noxious vapor. He sucked on the fumes. "Sweetness," he said. "Can't you hear the summer sparrows, the hummingbirds, the marching of the ants?" The house shifted perceptibly in the rush of yellow gas as it sought to escape. It clotted in the cracks under the windows. It condensed on the walls, rolling down in a steady brown drool. Branwell burped a red belch of steam. Pom Pom Pom, he said. And, by the time we made it back down the stairs, our ears rang.

Tabby coughed and gagged, "What kind of spice is that Master Branwell?"

His arms seemed thinner and more emaciated than the thin glass cylinder he held to his mouth. He stuck his tongue down the shaft as he inhaled the burning clay. Pom Pom Pom, he said. "Chinese spice." He closed the door.

Tabby by this time had opened all of the doors and windows. Snow blew in. The white powder mixed with the yellow dust leaving a brown paste on the flagstones in the entryway. We set to work then rubbing every surface down with cloths and water and ammonia. A quiet feeling settled over us, a sort of laziness, until Emily said, "I want to show you something." In the front yard, we could see up to Branwell's room and his magic lantern revolved and cast red spheres of moons, triangles of white stars, and hoops of green Saturns onto his window pane. His window sparked and shifted. Emily was the first to do it. She lay in the powdered snow in the front yard and made an angel by flapping her arms. We all lay in the snow staring up toward the dark sky watching each fleck coming down. I don't know how long we lay there more pleased and distracted than anyone has any right to be because the cold snow felt soothing on our burning skin, and the flakes of snow floated out of the blackness and took so, so long to get down out of sight.

Emily leaned forward, her face blue from the cold. "I feel funny," she said. She was sick in the snow. We all were sick in the snow. I vomited a thick inky chowder. I was surprised out how hot and viscous this substance was coming out compared to the thin gruel that went in. I wondered what else came out with it, dissolved liver and kidney and bone? We crawled back inside across the icy flagstones and back into the parlor and sat beside the fire. The house was frozen now. It smelled like ammonia and our cleaning. The bare walls and the dark flagstones were desolate. The wind outside blew unrelenting against the house. The fire did nothing more than heat our clothes and skin but could do nothing to scour the coldness in the pits of our empty stomachs.

Branwell was a constant danger to himself and others.

Shortly thereafter, he set himself on fire. This time the smoke was black, and the smell of burning clothes permeated the house. His bed burned and issued a slow and heavy smoke. His tobacco pipe had slipped free from his hands when he nodded off. When we noticed the smoke, we said, "Oh no, here it is again."

Tabby said, "Oh no, nothing. Not when I have to clean it up." She grabbed my washbasin. We followed her into his room, a jumble of newspaper, and crumpled balls of writing paper and crates and blankets. It looked like Branwell lay on a cloud, so much smoke came out of his bed. "Master Branwell, your bed is on fire," Tabby said.

He started to wake and then looked at us. "What are you doing in my room?"

"You are on fire you eejut." Tabby said and then doused Branwell and the bed with the basin. He didn't move, but lay in the soaked fabric, gray ash in his beard, stunned.

Branwell's handwriting failed over the years until he had distorted Glass Town's carefully formulated miniscule to a childlike block printing that he himself had trouble reading. He would sometimes demand that we read his latest composition, waving the piece of paper with the tiny marks from the top of the stairs. "This is a sonnet I wrote." He checked his pocket watch and then checked it again, "half an hour ago." He would try to read it and finally come down the stairs. "Charlotte, you are an excellent reader. Can you make this out?"

We sat with Branwell in his wrecked room. "Branwell, we are going to have to start some rules now."

He sat up. "About bloody time."

"You will have to follow these rules."

"I am a grown boy," he said. "A worthless sort, but grown damnit."

"Grown men don't urinate their pajamas," I said.

So he slept with Papa until he knew he would die. That last long month the house was quiet. We would visit him upstairs. He turned his head away from us. "I'm grown am I? I won't stand for you." Until finally when he wanted to stand, he could not even raise himself from the bed. "A cloud has crept into my vision, and it is making me dizzy. It is the color of a fawn, deep yellow with white spots." He could see it coming around the edge of his vision. "A rot," he said. He wanted to stand one last time to meet his death because "Let me face it sisters, I have been pretty damn lazy for a long time. I will stand before it comes. I will stand."

I say: Graphomania

The Brontës created the tiny size of their script to resemble the printed typeface for the books to be read by their toy soldiers, The Young Men, who lived in Branwell's toy city, Glass Town. This toy town persisted in the Brontë's life well beyond their adolescence. In fact, there was no real break between Branwell and Charlotte's Angrian writings and Emily and Anne's Gondall writings (the names of their respective childhood kingdoms) and the composition of their first mature works in the mid-1840s. The use of the minuscule script had become inseparable from the writing of fiction. The tiny script also conserved paper, which was not only expensive but difficult to obtain in Haworth.

Another effect of their tiny script was that it was very difficult to read for those not accustomed to it, and impossible to read by their father who suffered from very poor vision. For though they could be severely critical and sometimes poisonous in their sarcasm at each other's expense, to the world at large they presented a united and almost impenetrable front, which is a euphemistic way of saying they were quiet, shy, and unassuming, and who would guess that this plain woman hunched over a doll sized booklet was creating something like Heathcliff?

Emily says: Ellis

Sitting out on the moors in the dusk, I could smell the heather. The heather grew under the stones. The stones picked up the heat during the day. The heat that came down from the sun that kept hiding behind the clouds. The clouds that kept racing in the sky. I sat out with the stones, too, a dozen sheets of paper folded up in my pocket and my ink well and a pen and I listened to the wind come over the moors. The grass turned over and showed its silver undersides to the sky. I could see the wind coming from a long way off, a discoloration of the ground and then I leaned into the heavy stones like a warm brother out there in the middle of the sky and the hills, and the cold air brushed over me. The same air that carried the clouds to wherever they were going. I didn't like to write at home where Charlotte watched me. "What are you working on?"

"A letter."

"You must conserve yourself, Emily," she said. "You must conserve yourself for the writing session this evening. You do not want to be tired for the writing session this evening."

"I can rest between now and then. It is none of your business how I work."

So instead of fighting her, I walked out onto the moors and worked next to the large warm stones.

A stream ran down in the gully. I went down to get some water. Small flowers grew in the shrubs. The ruins of some dwelling that once stood in the hollow remained. Sometimes, if the wind were too strong, I sat next to it. This was my place. I hid my writing here. It sounds pitiable, the three of us sisters not even writing letters to distant people but writing to ourselves. This was the only constant company I knew these long years, myself. I read my former self and looked at the notes I left for myself, and I wondered how I would look back on this life here with my sisters and crippled father and dissipated brother years from now when I had gone on to find some respectable employment. Charlotte believed we would all be successful authors, but authors are not successful people to my understanding, as they all die poorly remembered, and it is a miracle we have their words at all. In this way, the words I wrote were a sad way to entertain myself.

I walked into Haworth sometimes to find company. I went to the stationary store and Robert Chambers smiled at me because I was there without Charlotte. He told me this. "When your sister comes, it means the next day I will have to make the trip into Keighley to purchase more paper. It is a wonder the quantity of paper your sisters and you use, Miss Brontë. You must write dozens of letters a week." I held my hand up to show him my callous, which I am very proud of because it is much larger even than Anne's and hers is larger than Charlotte's. Charlotte tells us that it is not an indication of anything except that we hold our pens too tightly, but I tell her the tightness of my pen is a matter of inspiration.

"I hardly think such a disfigurement merits anything except chastisement for a lack of disciplined penmanship," Charlotte said.

Sometimes when I come home early, I know she has gone through my belongings looking for whatever I am writing. That is how she found my poetry in the first place. Snooping about in my personal belongings. What is Charlotte's is hers and what is ours is Charlotte's. When Anne and I found a publisher for our first books and the publisher declined Charlotte's, she didn't seem angry even though Anne told me she expected Charlotte not to eat for a week. Instead Charlotte said, "The Brothers Bells have a publisher. I shall write another book to get Currer an even better one!"

Charlotte was cheerful. She said Ellis, and Acton's books had finally been reviewed. When our books finally came out, riddled with errors, printer mistakes, and dutiful transcription of obvious verbal ticks, everyone assumed that the Brother's Bell were the work of a single man. Does it indeed take three women nowadays to make one man? Charlotte laughed as she read us the review. I asked not to hear it, as I did not feel well, but she read it anyway, and because Charlotte was in such good spirits, I thought it must be a good review.

Acton, when left together to his own imagination, seems to take a morose satisfaction in developing a complete science of human brutality. In *Wuthering Heights* he has succeeded in reaching the summit of this laudable ambition. He details all the ingenuity of animal malignity, and exhausts the whole rhetoric of stupid blasphemy, in order that there may be no mistake as to the kind of person he intends to hold up to popular gaze. Nightmares and dreams, through which devils dance and wolves howl, make bad novels.

She said, "Isn't this delightful?"

I felt my face turn color. Tabby helped me up the stairs. Charlotte came to sit with me later. She didn't say anything, despite my pallor. I could see my reflection in the widow. When I coughed, she held a napkin to my mouth and concealed from me whatever I had coughed up.

Charlotte brushed my hand and then drew back. "You are so cold, Emily. It chills me to the bone just to touch you. You must be suffering horribly."

I nodded my head. "It is lovely weather for a walk."

"It is raining."

"I enjoy the rain."

"No wonder you are so ill."

The washing pitcher was too heavy for me to lift. I tipped it and poured a little water onto a cloth. I wiped the cloth over my skin. I dressed in clothes Anne had aired outside. I was not allowed outside anymore. When I smelled the fabric, I could smell the air and the wind and distant heather and I felt as close as I was likely to, to roaming across the grass and up to the lip of the hill where I could see everything. My legs ached from missed walks. Once I was dressed, I walked down the stairs and I was exhausted. It had been raining for over a month, and my lungs felt heavy. Out on the moors, the letters to myself were rotting, I was certain, turning into a fold of mushrooms and algae and moss. I had to stay up and moving because I did not want to go back to sleep and lose this day. Nothing was happening on this day. But dead, even nothing was something. So many days passed. I sat up in bed. The light came through my window, and I thought I should get someone to go get those letters and I could read them before I was gone because they were meant for me.

Charlotte says: Papa,
I am the bestselling author Currer Bell

When demand for the work had assured me of the success of *Jane Eyre*, Emily and Anne urged me to tell Papa of its publication. I went to his study one afternoon after his early dinner, carrying with me a copy of the book with two reviews, taking care to include notices adverse to it.

"Papa, I've been writing a book."

"Have you, my dear?"

"Yes, and I want you to read it."

"I am afraid it will try my eyes too much."

"But it is not in manuscript. It is printed."

"My dear! You've never thought of the expense it will be! It will almost be sure to be a loss, for how can you get a book sold? No one knows you or your name."

"But Papa, I don't think it will be a loss; no more will you, if you will let me read a review or two, and tell you more about it."

I sat down and read some of the reviews to Papa. I gave him a copy of *Jane Eyre* and left him to read it.

When I came into the parlor, Emily and Anne asked me, "Did you tell him?"

"I did."

"What did you say to him?"

"I told him *Jane Eyre* had been published and well received."

"Is that all you said to him?"

"I told him all there was to tell. It just remains for him to read my book."

When he came to tea later, Papa said, "Girls, do you know Charlotte has been writing a book? And it is much better than likely?"

"Papa," Emily exclaimed, "Anne and I have also published books."

"Indeed. Indeed. I shall go blind reading all of the books my girls are writing. Have you sold as many copies as Charlotte? She has developed quite a following."

"No, Papa," Emily said. Anne folded her napkin.

Anne says: [CENSORED]

"Words suppressed for your protection"
—Charlotte Brontë.

Please refer to the authorized edition of *The Life of Charlotte Brontë* by Elizabeth Gaskell.

After I finished my indoor chores at nine o'clock, Mr. Nicholls returned and went upstairs to his room. He said he felt awkward sitting in the parlor to witness my nightly ritual of composition. Ever since the three of us sisters had been very young, at nine o'clock we put away our housework and sat down to write. Father even forbad there to be curtains in the parlor because we burned so many candles working. At nine o' clock, he locked the front door and put out the lights and kissed me on my forehead.

"That was a stubborn thing you did today exposing yourself to the elements."

"The windows are washed now."

"But they will get dirty again this week and if you die of exposure, you will be dead forever."

I didn't matter. Just as my sisters didn't matter. We were alone except for our family in this world, and our presence mattered only in our own limited sphere. I worked at the table on my writing. My manner of composition, I should note, I have found slightly different than other writers. My works accumulate, each sentence fully cast, and then evaluated in the context of the whole. I throw down a sentence I think will advance the work and consider it and then strike it out, or more often than not go to the next as yet unwritten sentence. Sometimes these sentences are as difficult to cast as passing a kidney stone, and I wander around the table in a circle where years ago my two other dear sisters also wandered. We bumped into each other as we struggled with these thoughts, and the mutual struggle of us three helped us along. I could ask Emily a question, and she would be grateful for the escape from her labors, or I would listen to her explain her problem, often finding that in removing the weight of all the words I had accumulated that the solution would present itself to me. In this way, each step forward became more and more difficult until I reached the end.

I felt a little feverish before going to bed. I climbed the stairs, washed myself, and finally lay down. I listened to my father snoring in the other room. Mr. Nicholls' light was still on. When he heard me lay down in bed, he knocked. "Hello," he said.

"Hello," I said.

"How are you feeling?"

"I am feeling," I said, "A little tired."

I say: Words are the slime trails of the living

C harlotte writes down Emily's last words in her journal and writes down Anne's last words in her journal and rewrites them for posterity.

Charlotte says: The Dead can aspire to perfection;
we can rewrite them.

The living are a bottle neck to the memory of the dead. The dead remain with us in memory but we are faulty reservoirs for remembering how things were because we are subject to petty grievances, annoyances, and prejudices. I felt a chill setting inside my bones, an ice that would not melt in the boiling water Tabby poured over my skin. "You know better than to tempt, fate, dear," she scolded. "What with me recovering from the TB." The living themselves do not have a long memory of the dead as they also pass along, leaving behind notes and novels and heaps of trash. Yet, these words do not measure Emily or Anne or Branwell or myself. I have burnt my tracks and die unknown. I watched Tabby in the reflection of the window as she folded up her clothes and lugged the pail of water into the hallway. At night, the windows are mirrors. During the day, I can look out and at night the outside can look in on me.

www.ingramcontent.com/pod-product-compliance
Lightning Source LLC
Chambersburg PA
CBHW020617250626
47154CB00004B/1554